Before it began, the honeymoon was over!

Sabina had thought that David couldn't face making love to her because of the ugly scar on her face. Now she knew that he had married her only out of a sense of chivalry.

And yet, she knew, the rift between them was partly of her making. She had changed since the accident. Instead of the fun-loving, outgoing person she had been, she now shied away from meeting people. Somehow she felt she could never be happy until the scar on her face was removed.

How could David bear to touch her, when he had Shani pursuing him— Shani, so young and beautiful, so vibrant and alive and so much in love with him?

Other titles by
KATRINA BRITT
IN HARLEQUIN ROMANCES

Other titles by
KATRINA BRITT
IN HARLEQUIN PRESENTS

Many of these titles are available at your local bookseller
or through the Harlequin Reader Service.

For a free catalogue listing all available Harlequin Romances,
send your name and address to:

HARLEQUIN READER SERVICE,
M.P.O. Box 707, Niagara Falls, N.Y. 14302
Canadian address: Stratford, Ontario, Canada N5A 6W2

or use coupon at back of book.

The Midnight Sun

by

KATRINA BRITT

Harlequin Books

TORONTO • LONDON • NEW YORK • AMSTERDAM
SYDNEY • HAMBURG • PARIS

Original hardcover edition published in 1979
by Mills & Boon Limited

ISBN 0-373-02269-7

Harlequin edition published July 1979

Printed in U.S.A.

CHAPTER ONE

ENCHANTED, Sabina saw the last of the clouds disperse below the plane to reveal the silver surface of a lake in a frame of pines. The light and shade of green forests and crystal waters presented the grandeur of nature in all its glory. The scene was so relaxing, so beautiful that she could almost smell the pine-scented air. Yet her heart was heavy as she closed her eyes, leaned back in her seat and wound nervous slim fingers around the buckle of her seat belt.

No need to look at the band of gold below the exquisite engagement ring on her finger. It was as new as the charming outfit she wore and as heavy as her heart. Sabina was as acutely aware of it as the tanned, long-limbed, loose-jointed figure of the man seated beside her—David, her husband. Why, oh, why had she let him talk her into marrying him so soon after her accident when she had been so determined to stay single until the scar on her face had been dealt with and erased?

So much had happened in too little time—meeting David, the whirlwind courtship, then the car accident near to the London restaurant where they had arranged to meet to discuss the final arrangements of their wedding. Was it only six months ago that David strode into her life, turning all its drab colours into exciting rainbow hues which had dazzled and, at the same time, frightened her a little?

She had been delving into a box of bric-à-brac in an

antique shop in the West End of London, long slim legs encased in high white leather boots, willowy figure straightening in slender suppleness at the sound of his deep brown voice.

'Excuse me, I wonder if you can help me. I'm looking for a present for my aunt, a kind of Austrian fan by special request. She collects such things.'

His swift keen perusal of her as she straightened to face him had nothing cursory about it. Sabina had gazed at him with large clear eyes as he was speaking, staring at him. His lean face, more striking than good-looking, twitched in amusement as he addressed her. Crisp black hair, slightly ruffled, an alarmingly interesting mouth lifting at the corners, and dark brown eyes, almost black, which looked directly at her.

He really was very attractive, she had thought, with those intelligent dark eyes taking in the basalt jug she had been holding in slim, pearl-tipped fingers. It had proved quite an effort to find her voice beneath all that battery of charm. But she had managed it.

'I'm afraid I can't help you,' she had begun soberly until the wicked gleam in his eyes had brought a twinkle to her blue ones. 'Madame has just popped out. You know how it is—the dust from antiques is apt to dry and irritate the throat. She'll soon be back.'

His dark brows had arched in amusement as he had comprehended and Sabina had been aware of his slow perusal of her skin tanned to a light gold by brief modelling jobs in the sun, before wandering down to her tapering fingers as they set down the jug rather nervously. Resolutely, she had told herself that whether she was married or not was no concern of his. But he had intrigued her.

'I'll wait.'

He spoke in the manner of a man who made quick decisions and Sabina smiled, with the slanting rays of the sun through the window giving her a delicacy of features and form.

'I was asked to stay in the shop until Madame returns. I'm sure she'll find exactly what you want,' she had told him.

He had strolled around then and Sabina had tried to ignore the width of immaculate shoulders occasionally shutting out the light. She had left the shop immediately on Madame's return, only to bump into the man again on the evening of the same day. A sudden shower of rain after work had sent her hurrying along the crowded pavement with her face bent against the onslaught. They had collided head on.

Slim in her belted white raincoat, the hood of it pulled up over her bright hair, she had gazed up at him with raindrops sparkling on her eyelashes, and laughed. That second encounter set the seal on their future relationship. Within a very short time Sabina had been completely under David's spell. In fact she had fallen in love with him with an intensity that was frightening, and she knew as little about him as he knew about her.

His friends? A lively pot-pourri of professional people, some of whom she had met without learning anything more about him than she already knew. He was charming, popular with both sexes and he knew how to make a woman feel special and wanted. His nearness by her side forced her to recall the feeling of his strong arms around her, his dark eyes laughing down into hers, the touch of firm cool lips on her own.

'Penny for them, my sweet,' David drawled in a

leisurely almost casual ease of manner which was oddly comforting.

Sabina felt involuntarily that there was nothing to worry about. But she had been too deep in thought for his words not to startle her. He saw it and smiled with a flash of white teeth in his brown face. A firm brown hand sought hers and closed on them reassuringly.

'Relax, my pet. You're not to worry.'

Sabina found herself blushing, for there was now more meaning in his glances than there had ever been before. He was her husband and they belonged to each other. Married life for them was just beginning and she was thankful that they shared the gift of making a long silence seem companionable. David was not the restless type, easily bored. What restlessness he had was channelled into a disciplined grace which served to enhance his charm. If Sabina was restless, which she often was since the accident, he simply waited for her to adjust to his placid company and ease of manner which she so often felt hid a vein of steel in it.

Since the car crash Sabina had been constantly aware of the scar on her face. The other superficial bruises had healed quickly, thanks to her healthy body. There had been two operations on the scar on her left cheek and the last one was to come. The surgeon who had operated, a man of world-wide repute, was Finnish, and it had seemed like fate that his home should be in the vicinity of the place where they were to spend their honeymoon.

David, a consultant engineer, also had an appointment in the same lovely corner of Finland. It was something to do with the conservation of energy. So three projects were to be rolled into one—their honeymoon, David's new assignment and her final operation. David had wanted a honeymoon in the sun which he felt Sabina needed and had been against coming to Finland, preferring to leave his new assignment until the honeymoon was over.

But Sabina had been adamant. Until her scar had gone she wanted to stay somewhere quiet where she could go about unnoticed. It had, indeed, been one of the reasons for her consenting to get married so soon. Another had been her father's remarriage, too soon, Sabina felt, after her mother had died, to a woman she could not get on with.

For a long moment the scar on her face was forgotten as she sat, head back with her eyes closed. The bright hair fell away from her face to reveal the delicate moulding of her cheekbones. She would never be beautiful even when the scar had gone, for her features, though pleasing, were not outstanding. Her only claim to beauty was in the abundant bright hair like ripe corn and her wide-spaced blue eyes which, clear and sparkling, were always on the edge of laughter.

Five foot three in height with slim shapely legs and dainty feet which must always be clad in high heels to combat David's six foot odd, Sabina had enjoyed her quota of boy-friends, though none had been like David. She adored him, and the knowledge that he belonged to her now filled her with wonder and delight. She would never understand why he had chosen her from a woman's world which surely had been his oyster.

She was grateful for David's warm expression, denoting that his study of her face and form was very satisfactory. She was sitting by the window of the plane and her scarred cheek was that side, so he was spared the ordeal of looking at it. Not that he appeared to notice it.

Sabina quelled a shudder at the thought that the final operation might not be successful. David scoffed at her fears, but they were very real to her.

The trouble was her shyness where he was concerned. They knew so little about each other. Consequently she was hypersensitive where he was concerned, and the wretched scar made things no easier. Tentatively, she raised a hand to touch it as David spoke close to her ear.

'We're almost there. Tired?'

'Not very.'

She was too tensed up to feel tired or anything. Indeed her dread of the journey ending had only served to make the time go more quickly. She was sorely tempted to put her head on his shoulder to feel the comfort of his strength, but that would leave her scarred cheek uppermost and David had a habit of moving a hand caressingly over her flushed cheeks. It would be terrible to feel his sudden reaction when those long brown fingers came in contact with the ugly blemish on the smooth skin.

'I'll be thinking of you, Sabbie,' her brother Blair had promised her at the wedding. He had been best man. An up-and-coming photographer, he had taken the wedding pictures, making sure that her scarred cheek was hidden from the camera by taking her smiling up at David with her unblemished cheek to the camera.

She owed a lot to Blair whose excellent photography had been the means of her getting modelling jobs. At the age of twenty-two, she was on the verge of making a name for herself when David had come along. Now Sabina Farne was no more. She was Mrs David Savelon.

David leaned over, placed his lean hard brown cheek against her soft one and directed her gaze through the window.

'If you look a little to your left beyond the forest of pines you'll see the roof of the villa among the trees,' he said. 'See it?'

Sabina gazed down on a villa by a lake serene and lovely. She sighed.

'It looks fabulous,' she said. 'Those friends of yours are awfully kind to lease it to us.'

He grinned at her. 'Yes, aren't they? Sauna and all.'

Sabina felt her colour deepen beneath the steady gaze of mocking dark eyes.

'Isn't a sauna one of those places where you sit and perspire in your birthday suit while you beat yourselves with twigs or something?'

He chuckled at her rising colour. 'It's a natural way of life here, so don't look so shattered. This particular one is a small hut on the edge of the lake with two tiers of shelves around it for you to sit. After scrubbing yourself you sit on them while water is thrown on to white-hot stones to send up steam. Birching yourself with pliant twigs increases the circulation. Later, when the heat becomes intense and unbearable, you make a rush for an exhilarating jump in the cool waters of the lake.'

Sabina smiled. 'Sounds great, but rather embarrassing,' she said, and discovered the plane was losing height.

In no time at all under David's expert guidance they were on their way from the air-strip and greeting a tall fair man who awaited them beside his opulent car. He was sturdily built with a smile that showed strong white teeth in a not unattractive face.

'David, Sabina—welcome to my homeland. Also, I wish you much happiness in your marriage.'

Sabina had imagined Max Hiltunsen could give David, who was twenty-nine, at least five years. That had been when he had been attending to her at the hospital. This evening with the sun highlighting his blond hair and bulk in the immaculate suit he looked much younger. His eyes were as blue as the shirt he wore. His handshake was firm and cordial, his English almost free of accent.

He lost no time in putting their luggage in the car boot and soon they were on their way. Sabina, seated by David in the back of the car, gazed on the back of Max Hiltunsen with affection. At least there was one person here who could put her at her ease about her embarrassment over her scar. Like David he gave her the impression that it did not exist. Dear David!

Just then Sabina saw nothing but happiness in the years ahead as she clasped David's hand and shone up at him with all her love brimming over in her lovely eyes.

'Darling,' she whispered huskily, 'you aren't going to believe this, but I dreaded arriving here.'

Her words startled him somewhat, because the dark attractive eyebrows shot up in surprise.

'You did? But, my sweet, you wanted to come here. What were you afraid of? Not yours truly, I hope.'

He was laughing down at her with a look in his dark eyes which made her stomach turn over.

She said simply, 'I love you, David.'

He bent his head then to kiss her slightly parted lips as his arm stole around her.

'You're going to be ashamed of yourself, Mrs Savelon, for daring to be afraid of anything now that you're in my care.' He kissed her lips again in short kisses and spoke in between them to Max. 'What would you do with a wife like mine, Max?'

Max gave his attention to his driving and said slowly, 'I'm sure you don't need my advice. You are two people

very much in love, so there are no problems. Were I in
your shoes, David, I would still be wondering what I had
done to deserve Sabina.'

David laughed and gave her a final reassuring squeeze.
Dreamily, Sabina gazed out at the passing scenery as the
road followed the contours of lakes that gave an enchanting vista of gleaming water, beautiful trees and farms.
There was little traffic on the road, one or two farm
tractors, then children skipping home from school.

Presently the car swerved to the right to a gleam of
water visible between the trees and there was the villa.
David was out of the car first in one fluid movement.
Then Sabina was standing beside him, finding the crystal
clear air the sweetest she had ever breathed. In silence
she stared at the villa built stoutly of pinewood, loving
the deep eaves and the overall atmosphere of peace
broken only by the sweet trilling of birds.

She was thinking that this was to be a temporary home
for David and herself in which they would live as man and
wife for the first time. It was here in these beautiful
surroundings that the foundations of their future life
together would be laid. Her scarred face was forgotten in
a feeling of utter bliss.

'Oh, David, it's out of this world!' she breathed. 'And
just look at the lake, all our own.'

His arm was around her. 'A perfect spot for a honeymoon couple, isn't it? No one to disturb us.'

He laughed at the sudden rush of colour to her cheeks
as Max took their luggage from the car boot. Then
Sabina was laughing too, a sweet husky laugh of fresh
spring water trickling over stones.

'It is good to hear you laugh, Sabina. Keep it up. A
good laugh is the finest tonic in the world.'

Max was there, and she looked up at him, aware of the scar being visible to him on her left side. But she did not feel embarrassed for him to see it. Gazing on disfigurement was part of his daily life. Thank heaven for Max, she thought.

'We're being welcomed to the villa.'

David dropped his arm from Sabina's shoulders as a couple appeared at the door. The sun shone on their fair heads and their teeth showed white in a broad smile.

Max said easily, 'I believe you have already made the acquaintance of Eila and Leif Pihlstrum, David, who look after the villa.'

David nodded. 'Yes, indeed. I stayed here for a few days with the owners, Nigel and Emma Somers, while I was being interviewed for my present job. Then, learning of my forthcoming marriage, they very kindly offered to lease me the villa while they were away in America.'

'A charming couple, the Somers,' Max commented. 'As are Eila and Leif. I am sure you will both be very happy here.'

Eila and Leif were now directly in front of them, Eila with her fine precise features framed enchantingly in golden braids of hair, Leif with his pale hair and expressive dark eyes beside her.

David introduced them to Sabina with his easy charm of manner that put them immediately at their ease. They greeted her unexpectedly in slow precise English, then Leif took their luggage upstairs and Max said regretfully that he must leave them.

He said, 'Mother would be delighted if you would both dine with us one evening. If you will so honour us with your company.' His eyes twinkled. 'We must not forget that you are on your honeymoon, so perhaps you will let us know when it is convenient.'

David clasped his hand. 'We shall be delighted. When I've discovered what arrangements my colleagues here have made, we'll let you know.'

The interior of the villa was cool, for the picturesque stove reaching for the high ceiling was unlighted. It dominated a pleasant room with its colourful tiles depicting scenes of country life that lent an air of gaiety to the pine-covered walls disguising precious storing space. The pine table and chairs with their brightly coloured cushions, the sewing machine in one corner and an overhanging lamp gave the impression of a room well used.

Not so the salon adjoining it, with its dining annexe and windows overlooking the grounds of the villa. It seemed to Sabina as she entered it with Eila that it was like an old lady who had sailed unscathed through the ravages of years—an old lady who still contrived to look beautiful in faded silks, brocades and precious taffetas. Cabinets of precious porcelain, exquisite watercolours on the walls, lights dancing on crystal chandeliers and ornate mirrors gave an air of gracious living.

Sabina shone up at David. 'Isn't it adorable? It's perfect, isn't it?'

Looking down at her glowing eyes and pink parted lips, he said gravely, 'It is with you in it.'

Eila laughed. 'That is what I call a compliment, Mrs Savelon. I am so pleased that you find it to your liking. And now before I take you to your rooms, I have a message for you, Mr Savelon, from someone named Urfo Mikkola. He telephoned and I wrote the message down.'

She gave David a note from the pocket of her apron and he scanned it quickly with a frown.

His smile at Sabina was rueful. 'Sorry, my sweet. I have to go out to meet my colleagues—something has come up, an urgent matter by the looks of it, and they want my opinion. Look, I know you're tired with the journey, so why not go to bed after you've eaten? I'll try to get back as soon as I can.' He drew a lean hand on the thick dark hair as he thrust an arm around her slender figure. 'You know what?' he added. 'I forgot to carry you over the threshold.'

Sabina swallowed on a dry throat and managed a gallant smile. 'It doesn't matter, because this isn't our real home. I understand about this job of yours. I'll be all right. I think I'm tired.'

Eila broke in quickly, 'I can bring a tray to your room, Mrs Savelon. As for Mr Savelon, I have the keys to the car in the garage which I have been instructed to hand over to you. I believe you used it when you were here before.'

'That's right, I did. That's great. Come on, darling, I'll carry you to our rooms. It's the least I can do.'

David suited the action to the word and scooping Sabina up in his arms he strode from the salon and carried her up the stairs. Eila was evidently the romantic kind, for she followed them with a delighted smile, rushing before them to open the door of their rooms.

As he sat Sabina gently down his eyes alighted on their luggage on the carpet.

'Don't bother to unpack for me, my sweet. I'll do it when I come back.' Suddenly he gave a devilish grin. 'Urfo suggests we discuss matters in a sauna so I'll make do with a quick wash and change.'

When he had gone into his dressing room with his case Sabina opened her own. Eila had gone downstairs. Her offer to help unpack had been gently turned down by Sabina, who did not take long to empty her case since there was a surfeit of cupboards and drawers to accommodate her clothes.

Their rooms comprised a large bedroom with a bathroom and adjoining dressing room leading off. The décor was based on the Aubusson carpet with its delicate colours echoed in the high carved ceiling and walls. Lace blinds at the tall windows were the same fabric as the bedspread. A beautiful, restful room, Sabina felt in all her tiredness. She had slipped out of her suit and was belting a wrap around her when David came ready to go out.

He strode in bringing with him a faint aroma of sandalwood soap. His face was cool from his recent wash, his lean tanned cheek hard against her soft one as he hugged her then kissed her briefly.

'This is awful,' he groaned. 'Tearing myself away from you like this. But we'll make up for it.'

Then he was gone.

Sabina had washed under the shower in the bathroom and had put on her nightdress and wrap when Eila arrived with her supper on a tray.

'Please get into bed, Mrs Savelon, and spoil yourself. You will enjoy your food much better as you relax between the sheets. I hope what I have prepared will please you. There is one thing I must mention. We do not have a surfeit of green vegetables in our country, but Leif grows them in the garden. Mrs Somers started it when she bought the villa. Our main diet through the years has been based on grain, meat, fish and fats with very little green vegetables.'

Sabina obediently sat up in bed to accept the covered tray across her knees.

'The food smells delicious,' she said warmly as Eila took the cover off a silver dish of soup. 'What does Leif do apart from helping you keep house, Eila?'

'He distributes the mail. He is also working for his

degree in engineering in Helsinki. So you can imagine how thrilled he is to have your husband stay here in the villa.' Her eyes were anxious as Sabina tried the soup. 'You like it?'

Sabina set the spoon to her lips, then nodded. 'Hmm, delicious. Vegetable?'

Eila nodded, well satisfied. 'Carrots and turnips with our own special flavouring.'

'Do you do all the cooking, Eila?'

'My husband can cook as well as I can. We have been married for two years. He had a widowed mother and two small brothers to support, so he left school early in order to get a job and earn money for their keep. Two years ago his mother married again, a well-to-do business man in Helsinki, so Leif was free to marry me. I hope you will be as happy as Leif and I have been.'

'I hope so too.' Sabina had enjoyed the soup and she put down her spoon for Eila to remove the empty dish. 'I suppose you know about my scar?' She lifted a hand and pushed the bright hair from her scarred cheek, and added, 'Don't tell me that you haven't noticed it.'

Eila surveyed the scar dispassionately and shrugged with scarcely a change of expression.

She said, 'Does it bother you?'

'Of course. It's dreadful!'

Eila removed the empty soup plate and placed a second dish in front of her, saying philosophically, 'I would not say that it is dreadful. It is overshadowed by your beautiful eyes.'

'You're very kind, Eila, and I love you for it, but the scar remains.'

Eila's voice had a ring of firmness about it. 'Then you must keep it in its rightful place—on your face and not on your mind. Forgive me for being personal, but is Mr Hiltunsen interested in it?'

'Yes. He's confident that he can erase it.'

'Then if he says so he will. Our men are industrious and shy, but they never boast. Mr Hiltunsen is a very clever surgeon. One moment he will tell you that something is impossible and the next will find him doing it in his modest way. You are fortunate to have his services. Do you mind telling me how it happened?'

'My husband and I had arranged to meet at a restaurant in London to discuss the final arrangements for our wedding. I arrived minutes before he did. In those few minutes a car went out of control across the road and I was hit by flying glass. David arrived at the same time as the ambulance.'

Eila nodded comprehendingly. Her voice was not without concern.

'How dreadful for you, but we must be thankful that it was not worse. Is Mr Hiltunsen to do the operation here in Helsinki?'

'I've no idea. He wants me to recuperate first. It was a shattering experience.'

'I'm sure it was, but what nicer way to recuperate than on a honeymoon—especially when the bridegroom is as charming as Mr Savelon! He will take care of you,' Eila said placatingly.

'Is Mr Hiltunsen married?' Sabina asked curiously.

'No. He lives with his mother across the lake. You can see his villa from the window. You heard me mention Mr Urfo Mikkola just now? Mr Hiltunsen was once engaged to his sister, Kirsty. She was quite plain but nice, and everyone was surprised when Mr Hiltunsen chose her from the many beautiful women he knew. Then suddenly

the engagement was broken off and Kirsty left to go
nursing in a hospital in Helsinki.'

'What happened?'

'No one was quite clear about it, but I had a good idea.
However, it is none of my business. All I know is that two
nice people were parted and neither has found anyone
else.'

Sabina's appetite was broken, mostly by tiredness, but
the presence of Eila and her anxiety to please persuaded
her to try a little of the courses specially cooked for her.
She ate a generous portion of the stewed meats accompanied by boiled potatoes and turnips, tried and found
delicious the crisp pancake which followed, filled with
rice, and insisted upon Eila joining her in a cup of the
excellent coffee which she brought.

It was comforting to know that Eila was a person she
could like and trust. They had more conversation,
Sabina seeking to know something of what was expected
of her during her stay. When she asked about the sauna
Eila smiled.

'You don't have to use it if you don't want to. On the
other hand, I see no reason why you should not enjoy it.'
Her eyes twinkled as she paused, then added, 'I think it is
the idea of being in the nude that embarrasses you, but
you need have no qualms about it. After all, the steam
makes you partly invisible and the bath house is so near
to the lake that you can plunge in without anyone around
being aware of it.'

To cover her self-consciousness, Sabina said brightly,
'I'm a little shy yet of my husband, so I'll try the sauna
on my own to begin with.'

'As you wish. I will show you how it is done when you
are ready. But with your figure you have nothing to

worry about, and it is indeed a grand way of keeping fit.'

Sabina lay quietly with her eyes on the ceiling when Eila had gone. She was thankful for the respite and the chance to rest. The incident of the car crash on that fateful day had torn her nerves somewhat and the extra tension incurred through her marriage was no help. However much she had been against marrying David so soon it was possibly the most sensible thing to do. But she knew that it was not the answer to her present problems. The scar on her face stood between herself and her complete recovery. Not only was it a constant reminder of a shattering experience, it was a barrier between her and happiness. All the strain, uneasiness, and the inevitable feeling of being the target of sympathetic and curious eyes would be there until the scar was removed. She certainly did not feel as a bride on her first night should do—eager for her husband's arms. The panicky conviction was there that the scar would affect him as well. She could almost feel her tension as those cool lips of his moved around her neck and face, nearing the scar.

She pushed the bright hair back from a damp forehead. There must be no panic. Thank goodness she had used her common sense and eaten before retiring. It had not been the most sensible thing to do to induce sleep, but it did subdue the quivery feeling inside her since the wedding. Her eyes closed. There was complete silence. The bed was comfortable, the sheets freshly impregnated with clean pine air. Slowly, Sabina turned to lie on her side and face the other half of the bed which David would occupy when he returned. This was all wrong, she thought, remembering that here in Finland at this time of the year the sun shone all through the night. They should have dined together, David and herself. Then they should have taken a stroll beside the lake in the exciting phenomenon of a sun shining at midnight seemingly for them. Tears trickled between her lashes. Maybe she was not the only one to avoid what should have been all the endless joys of a wedding night.

Her thoughts became bemused. She was conscious only of David, whom she loved more than anyone else on earth. David whose immaculate grooming never entirely subdued the animal masculinity he seemed to convey. If she was not entirely fit herself there was no doubt about it that David was. He would love the sauna as he loved swimming, skiing, rugger and all the delights of sports in the open air. She wondered what he was doing at that moment—thinking about her? She doubted it. But her thoughts of him were so strong that he seemed to be there beside her. She could almost smell that faint pleasing aroma of cigars mixed with sandalwood soap which he used. His name was on her lips when sleep claimed her.

CHAPTER TWO

SABINA awoke feeling entirely refreshed to a room flooded with light. The curtains had remained undrawn, since the villa was not overlooked by other dwellings. The distance across the lake to similar villas was considerable and lace drapes did cover the window to give a minimum of privacy. Moving her head, she noticed two things at once, one that David had certainly not shared her bed during the night, two that there was a note for her propped up on the dressing table.

Quickly, because she wanted to keep waking problems at bay for a little while longer, Sabina reached for the silk wrap she had put in readiness the night before to slip over the wispy froth of a nightdress, and padded to the window.

The lake shimmered in the stillness and her eyes travelled across the stretch of water to a villa almost exactly opposite to her. Max Hiltunsen's villa. She wondered what his mother would be like and whether she had been the one to come between her son and the girl he had wanted to marry. If that was so then Sabina Savelon would never become one of her friends.

It was strange how the mind works, for in that instant even as she was musing over the affairs of Max it suddenly occurred to her that David might be sleeping in the dressing room. As swiftly as the thought had come she was across the room and turning the handle of the communicating door to open it gently. No sound. Moving slowly into the room she saw the evidence of him having spent the night there, or what part of it had been left when he returned. The divan had obviously been used as a bed, for the cushions were piled into a dented pillow at one end and his dressing gown was flung over the back of a chair.

He had unpacked his suitcase, for his clothes were on hangers in the wardrobe, a smart safari suit in beige, casuals, sports clothes and evening dress. David was nothing if not with-it. Sabina recalled the thick dark hair curling in the nape of his neck giving him that perfectly groomed appearance which he seemed to slip into naturally as though it was congenital like his good manners.

She had been agreeably surprised to discover that though he was an only child he had been too strong-willed to allow his mother to spoil him. When he had taken her home to meet his parents she had been alight with curiosity and interest. David had told her that his mother was an excellent cook and a charming hostess, but she was not to let it bother her. In fact, he had loved Sabina because her vitality and warmhearted outlook on life rendered her not too efficient to make mistakes. He could not bear clever women. They were apt, he said, to develop into the bossy type that he abhorred.

Her bones melted at the very thought of him and she went to pick up the note propped on the dressing table.

Darling, he had written, Sorry. Our discussion started in the sauna which my colleagues assured me was the best place since one can relax and talk quite freely. Unfortunately it went on without an agreement being reached between us. Can you imagine an American, a Finn and an Englishman arguing it out over the senseless ideas governments come up with. It seems the Finns are no different from anyone else in their opposing ideas to an excellent project. I returned in the early hours and decided to use the dressing room in case I wakened you from the sleep you so badly needed. You were still asleep this morning when I had to leave. We have to reach an agreement as quickly as possible because of the money loan needed for the project in hand. See you soon. All my love, David.

In other words, she thought hollowly, forget last night as if it had never been. Of course that was the sensible thing to do. Ever since the accident Sabina had sought to be tranquil, but beneath that hard-won tranquillity a cold fear clutched at her heart. Before, she had never been the hysterical kind. Now it seemed that she was never quite sure of her emotions. Maybe a session under the shower would help.

In the bathroom David's shaving tackle and hair-brushes gave her a feeling of belonging, and when she finally emerged in her wrap Eila came with a drink.

Eyes twinkling, she said, 'What about trying the sauna since your husband is out! I will take you through the processes and if you do not wish to jump into the lake there is always a pan handy to douse yourself in cold water.'

So Sabina tried the sauna, sitting high above the hot stones while Eila poured water on them to induce steam. Then the twigs were used to invigorate her body. She enjoyed the sudden dive into the lake which followed. There was no feeling quite like it, she assured a smiling Eila when later she sat down to breakfast feeling fit and glowing with health.

Eila, looking with satisfaction at her glowing face and

bright clear eyes, voiced her approval. 'Already you are looking much better.'

Sabina watched as she sliced rye bread topped with poppy seeds, then put wads of golden butter into a dish. By now thoroughly at home with Sabina, she chatted on in her halting English.

'I had a word with Mr Savelon before he left this morning about the food. He is quite agreeable to eating Finnish dishes but referred me to you. How do you feel about it, Mrs Savelon? Green vegetables, fresh ones, are scarce early in the summer because we cannot do any winter sowing on account of the weather. Also our bread is different from yours.'

'That's all right. I shall enjoy Finnish food,' Sabina said warmly. 'I enjoyed the meal you gave me last evening and this bread looks delicious with the creamy yellow butter. After all, what's the use of visiting another country if you don't savour the way they live?'

'That is exactly what Mr Savelon said. It is good that you agree on things. He was not happy at having to leave you again today. He said he hoped to be back for the midday meal.'

'Which leaves me with the morning free.' Sabina hesitated before sinking her teeth in the rye bread and delicious butter. 'I noticed a boathouse by the lake. I wondered if there happens to be a boat on hand.'

'But certainly. Leif will prepare it for you. It is not too far for you to row across and you will find it very interesting on the other side. There is a restaurant where you can have a meal or a drink of tea or coffee. I would advise the tea since coffee is very expensive. We Finns usually have a light breakfast and the midday lunch can start as early as eleven-thirty in the morning.'

Sabina bit into her bread, munched, then answered the unspoken question in Eila's eyes.

'Shall we say lunch at one o'clock,' she said. 'Will that suit you? I'm thinking that it will give my husband time to return to the villa and perhaps have a wash and change.'

Eila smiled warmly, well pleased with her visitor for falling in with her routine. It was a pity, she thought, that a girl so newly married should be left to her own devices so much. And she did not look happy. There was a haunting expression in her eyes which should not be there. Of course it was a rather unusual honeymoon with so much unfinished business related to it. But they made a very beautiful couple, he with his splendid physique and unending charm, she so sweet, so vulnerable and lonely. Later she watched Sabina walk gracefully down to the lake. Her golden hair, shoulder length, swung in a silky bright mass about her head. Her slim shoulders were square in the cream tailored silk blouse, and the matching cream linen skirt secured around her trim waist with an Otto Ganz belt revealed slim legs as she hoisted her shoulder bag into place.

Leif had the boat waiting and had supplied cushions from the villa. His shy smile showed strong perfect teeth.

'Sure you can manage on your own, Mrs Savelon?' he asked as he helped her on board.

'Yes, thanks. It's a lovely day. Thanks for the cushions.'

Sabina settled down in the middle of the boat and took hold of the oars. Leif pushed the boat out, stood for several minutes until he was satisfied that she was capable of handling it, then after lifting a hand, he strolled back towards the villa.

The water, smooth as silk, shimmered in the sun, and

the pines growing almost to the waters edge were refreshingly aromatic. Sabina did not intend to go far. It was the solitude she needed. The scenery was breathtaking and it would have been like Eden itself had David been with her. But she must not think of David until they met for lunch. The boat was in good repair, the oars moved easily, and Sabina felt that she could go on rowing for ever.

A small group of boys were sailing and swimming about with toy boats when she tied the boat up on the other side of the lake to a small jetty. The silk curtains of hair fell over her face as she secured the boat and she felt their eyes upon her. Mindful of the scar, she swept back her hair and turned her back to them to find someone blocking her path.

'Mrs Savelon.' Max Hiltunsen was smiling. 'I hope you will not mind me butting in like this, but when I saw you heading this way I felt that I had to come to see if I could be of any assistance.'

Sabina said warmly, 'That was very sweet of you and I appreciate it. Actually I was only going to browse around, maybe have a snack in the restaurant and then make my way leisurely back to the villa.'

'Why not come to see our villa? It is quite near. Besides, you will do better to shop when your husband is with you. He can pay for your purchases.'

He held her elbow lightly as they left the lakeside.

'David had to go out,' she said. 'It seems they're having trouble getting the project off the ground, as it were.'

He smiled reassuringly. 'Every new venture has its teething troubles. And nothing worth while is ever done in a hurry. How are you feeling? No nightmares?'

'No,' she answered laconically. No more nightmares of the accident, but nightmares of her approaching operation on the scar. But to tell him this would be to under-rate her faith in him as a surgeon. She could not hurt him, so she said brightly, 'I like your sauna baths.'

His eyes twinkled down at her. 'You have taken one with your husband?'

She felt her face go hot. 'No. David was out early this morning.'

'But you will. You will find it great fun—and do not look so shy. Never shrink from reality and nature. It is not healthy. Sharing a sauna with your husband will help you to shed some of those inhibitions of yours. You have a beautiful face and body. You should be proud of them. How do you imagine people who are born deformed go on?'

She laughed ruefully. 'I suppose you think me very self-centred.'

'Not a bit. You have come through a very shattering experience very well. However, you are alone far too much. It is not good for you to brood; I must have a talk with your husband.'

Sabina laid a hand on his arm and looked up at him in alarm.

'Please promise me you won't do that. It's my fault that David combined our honeymoon with work. He was all for me going away to some hot country to recuperate. I simply can't add to his troubles at the moment. It wouldn't be fair. This project he's on is an opening to greater things for him.'

'And what about your marriage? Is not that important?'

'Of course it is, and David would be the first to agree with me. But I won't have him upset because of me.'

'Then you must mix more with people and not spend so much time alone. What about coming to the hospital in Helsinki to look around? You would find it interesting.'

Sabina shrank inwardly. 'Not yet, if you don't mind. I shall enjoy myself looking around on my own.'

'Then come up to our villa for a coffee.'

'I haven't much time if I have to be back for lunch. Besides, I don't want to steal a march on David since he's more or less promised to dine with you some time.'

Max smiled tolerantly. 'Then you must not object to having coffee with me here in the restaurant,' he said firmly. 'I will take no refusal and since you have not been here before you will enjoy the novelty of it.'

Sabina did not demur but allowed him to escort her to the smart restaurant overlooking the lake. In one corner of the panelled room an attractive young man was playing *Rustle Of Spring* on a baby grand piano. Picturesque lamps hung low over immaculate tables and smart waitresses hovered with smiling faces.

Max ordered, then said, 'I have an account here. It is handy for me to bring my patients when I want to know more about them. My work requires a deep understanding of human nature.'

He went on to talk about Finland and the countless lakes, the enormous forests, once the hunting ground of Russian aristocracy. Time went on wings and Sabina rose reluctantly to go in order to be back at the villa in time for lunch.

He walked down with her to the boat, helped her in and pushed it off. Then he stood watching her row across for quite some time. As his figure dwindled in the distance he struck Sabina as being a lonely man, and she thought about the absent Kirsty.

On approaching the villa she saw a figure standing on the edge of the lake as though waiting for her. The girl was a stranger, but even at a distance there was something disturbing about her which Sabina could not explain. She was compellingly attractive with a tanned skin, large dark eyes and a thick cap of short black hair. As the boat scraped the shore Sabina saw that the girl was more attractive than pretty in a striking sort of way. Her nose was slightly curved, giving her features an appearance of being finely cut. She wore a sleeveless shirt over matching cream silk slacks and the bent arm holding a scarlet blazer over one shoulder was decorated with golden bangles. A careless arrogance hung about her like a cloak and her eyes were hard in one so young, for she could not have been more than seventeen. Those dark eyes were now fixed upon Sabina as though searching for something until they saw the scar. To Sabina that momentary glance could never be discounted nor forgotten.

She contrived a smile to meet that stony stare. 'Hello,' she said in her usual forthright friendly fashion.

The dark eyes were insolent. 'Sabina Farne?'

'Sabina Savelon. I was Sabina Farne. Should I know you?'

'So he married you after all?'

Something dark swept over the bright day as Sabina wrinkled a smooth forehead. 'Do you mean David?' she asked with a friendly smile.

'Who else? I don't suppose he told you about me. I'm Shani Somers. My parents own this villa.'

'This is rather unexpected, since I had no idea that the owners of the villa possessed a daughter. You're aware, of course, that your parents have leased the villa to us for three months?'

Sabina's smile did not get an answering one. The girl's expression was enigmatic.

'So David didn't tell you about me, about us?'

The last two words had an ominous ring about them
and Sabina went cold inside. The quiet air assumed a
listening quality and she moistened dry lips.

'Tell me what?' she asked slowly.

'That David came here a week before you married and
we fell in love.'

Sabina laughed. She looked such a child. 'You mean
you fell in love with David? How old are you, Shani?'

'Going on for eighteen.'

'So you had a crush on David. I know he paid a flying
visit here, but there was scarcely any time for him to have
a searing love affair since his time was taken up with conferences concerning his work. And he did marry me.'

Shani's nostrils quivered and her full mouth tightened
angrily.

'David married you from a sense of chivalry and the
fact that he felt responsible for your accident. What other
reason would a man like David marry himself to that?'

The gesture of her eyes and head to indicate the scar
on her cheek was cruelly scornful. Sabina retreated as
from a mortal blow and her hands clenched by her sides.

'David married me because he loved me,' she said
huskily. 'That's what marriage is all about, not a sudden
lust or a need for an affair. It's something far deeper than
that kind of thing. You'll learn all about it some day. I
had crushes on men at your age, most girls do, but they
never lasted long. It's a way of growing up and maturing.'

Sabina had spoken gently and without rancour, but
the effect of her words on Shani was startling. She was
almost beside herself with anger.

'Don't you dare talk to me as if I was a kid!' she
threatened. 'I know as much about love as you do.
Looked in a mirror lately? You'd better look again and

ask yourself what man would ever want to marry you unless, like David, he couldn't get out of it honourably.'

Sabina had managed to keep calm until now, but the barbed looks dipped in venom to which she was being subjected were as lethal as the cruel words. Her voice wavered as she spoke.

'You've made dreadful accusations concerning my husband, and I suggest you stay for lunch so that we can thrash this matter out once and for all. David will be here by then.'

Shani's self-assurance dropped somewhat as she said scornfully,

'And what would it prove? David would never admit his real reason for marrying you now. He'd probably call me a silly, starry-eyed kid and pass the whole thing off as a joke. You'll never know, will you, if he loves you or not?'

With this parting shot Shani turned on her heel and ran away from the villa towards the main road. Dazedly Sabina watched her go, with the feeling that the whole incident was a mere figment of her imagination. If only it was! But it had bitten too deeply into her emotions to be shrugged off as something unimportant. It left her shattered and cold, drained of all feeling yet quivering from head to toe.

She found herself looking at David through different eyes, his reluctance to come to Finland as part of their honeymoon, his returning home late the previous evening and using the spare room. His actions were suspect. Useless now to tell herself that his main concern had been for her welfare, that he wanted her to get fit again as quickly as possible.

Without being aware of it she was walking into the villa and turning her footsteps towards the kitchen quarters. The car was not outside, so David had not yet returned. She found Eila putting the finishing touches to an oval pastry with a cheese and rice filling, already baked to a golden brown; Eila was buttering it before putting it in a cloth to be served hot with more butter later.

She looked up as Sabina entered. 'Mr Savelon has not yet returned. Did you enjoy your outing on the lake?'

'Yes, thanks.' The other woman's warm smile helped to calm her frayed nerves. 'I've left the boat moored in case we want to use it again. Is that all right?'

Eila nodded and placed the buttered pastry into a cloth. 'Leif will always put it away at the end of the day,' she answered briskly.

'I didn't know that Mr and Mrs Somers had a daughter. I met her just now by the lake.'

'You met Shani here by the lake?' Eila looked up, startled. 'She has not been into the villa. Where is she now?'

'I've no idea. She just left. Why isn't she here at home? She's awfully young to be allowed to roam about.'

'Do not waste your sympathy on Shani, Mrs Savelon. If ever anyone was capable of taking care of themselves, she is. She is supposed to be staying with an aunt in Helsinki until her parents return home. You have no idea how she came here?'

Sabina shook her head. 'I saw no car, but it could have been waiting outside on the road.'

Eila nodded in agreement. 'Someone could have driven her here—she has plenty of young friends in Helsinki. She is at university but is now free from studies with the summer recess.'

'She's very attractive.' Sabina felt as though she was

speaking woodenly, but she had to know. 'I believe my husband met her when he paid a brief visit here just before our marriage.'

'Ah, yes. Shani was here from university for the week-end. Her parents wanted to take her with them to America, but she would not go, so they arranged for her to stay with the aunt in Helsinki.'

'But surely she would have been all right here? I mean, I know we had the lease, but she had you and your husband to keep an eye on her.'

'Mr and Mrs Somers thought it would not have been right for a third person to be here with a couple on their honeymoon.'

Sabina could not explain it, but suddenly Eila became guarded in a changed atmosphere. She watched her put the pastry away in a warm place and pick up prepared ingredients in a mixer to add milk.

Sabina said carefully, 'Strange that David never told me about her. He must have met her during his short stay here at the villa. I wonder why he never mentioned her.'

Eila plugged in the mixer and shrugged. 'He probably thought it was not important. He appeared to tease her a lot and regard her generally in the way one would a play-ful kitten. When Mr and Mrs Somers went away they decided to leave her in the care of an aunt in Helsinki because a relative has more influence and can chastise on occasions, which Leif and I could not do if Shani had been left in our charge.'

'I see,' Sabina replied, when all the time she did not. There had been no pleasure on Eila's face because the daughter of the house had called. Neither did she seem hurt because the girl had not bothered to call in to say hello. Something was wrong. What was more, Eila did not look at all happy to have Shani around.

'Do you like Shani, Eila?' she asked bluntly.

The other woman switched off the mixer but did not raise her head.

'Sometimes. There was a time not long ago when I did not like her. It is better for everyone that she is away.'

Sabina moistened dry lips. She was sorely tempted to confide in Eila, tell her what had passed between Shani and herself. But she could not for in doing so she would be implicating David. Servants gossiped like anyone else, and until she knew Eila better confidences were not to be thought of. However, there was no reason why she should not find out things for herself by diplomatic questioning.

'That time you mentioned when you did not like Shani, was my husband here then?'

'No. I would rather not talk about it.'

'I understand. I'll go and change. I hope my husband comes in time for our midday meal after you going to so much pains to prepare it.'

Eila relaxed visibly. 'He will come. I would say from experience that your husband is a man of his word. He will come—you will see.'

Sabina plunged a face still burning from her encounter with Shani in deliciously cool water in the bathroom. Then, patting it dry, she stepped into sandals and put on a simple cotton frock which fastened down the front with buttons shaped like rose petals to match the belt around her trim waist. The colour of the dress, a pretty shade of blue, brought out the deep blue of her eyes, and as she brushed the silky golden hair the thought occurred that Shani Somers and herself had nothing in common. As in their colouring, they were completely different.

She supposed that by now the girl would be well on her way back to Helsinki. I ought, Sabina thought with compunction, to have laughed at her and not got so het up about her childish insinuations. After all, it was her home and she could have insisted upon the girl staying to see David to repeat what she had told herself. It would have been far better to have dealt with the situation on the spot instead of letting it gnaw at her inside like a dog with a bone.

On the other hand, what was her own love for David worth if she did not trust him implicitly? The best thing to do was to forget the whole incident, even Shani's taunting look at her scarred face.

The sound of the car was followed very quickly by David himself striding into their room. He must have taken the stairs two at a time, but he showed no sign of quickened breathing when he strode across the room to enfold her in strong arms and place cool lips on hers.

'Sorry I'm late,' he said, releasing her and slackening his tie. 'I had to remind them that I was on my honeymoon and that my bride was waiting for me.'

He moved swiftly across the room while he talked into his dressing room. He took a quick shower and while he dressed Sabina gathered up the soiled towels and straightened the bathroom.

'Come on,' he said as he reappeared in light slacks, open-necked shirt and sandals. 'You and I have a lot of time to make up for.'

At lunch David was in the best of spirits, congratulating Eila on the lunch and the cheese and rice-buttered pastry which she told him was known as Karelian pastry. He winked at Sabina, told her to take note of it and asked what she had been doing that morning.

She told him about her row across the lake and her meeting with Max Hiltunsen.

'I didn't go with him to his villa to meet his mother because I want to go with you,' she confessed with a fond smile.

As always when she was with him she was under his spell. He had wooed her with a charm and skill that had completely captivated her, and if he had married her out of a sense of gallantry, as Shani said, he had never for a moment allowed her to suspect it.

Looking at him now, a picture of healthy, virile manhood, Sabina felt the same breathless excitement which he had always stirred in her from their first meeting. The eager anticipation with which she had looked forward to meeting him, the delights of being together in his car, dining with him, shouting with him at rugger matches, strolling with him in the park, chortling wickedly at bad plays and applauding the good ones. Many times when they reached the door of her flat after an evening out the laughter in her throat had only been silenced by his cool firm lips.

Small wonder that he had become part of her. But was she part of him? They had married in haste, but what of it? The beginning of their married life was no less real because of it. No one could have been kinder, more considerate. If there had been a lack of passion in the casual kisses he had given her since the wedding it had been because they had never actually been alone. And there was the scar. Since then he had treated her like a piece of Dresden china.

He was saying, 'You should have gone to meet Mrs Hiltunsen, my sweet. Max would probably tell her about your meeting and she might have sent him out to meet you, seeing that their villa gives such an unobstructed view of the lake.'

'You mean they might have both seen me rowing across? I never thought of that.' Sabina felt her face go hot while David fixed dark eyes upon her as if appraising the picture she made, her slender-waisted figure, her golden hair rioting in feathery tendrils about the warm sudden glow to her cheeks.

A slow smile curved his well cut lips. 'Not to worry. We aren't sure whether that did happen. What I'm trying to say is that just because I'm not available at the moment you aren't expected to stay at home until I am. Maybe I should have put you in the picture more. I would have done had I known what this visit would entail.'

'Would you, David?'

He looked at her then with the quizzical rising of a dark brow. 'I'm sorry,' he said quickly, 'I put that wrong. This is our honeymoon—and what a fiasco it's turning out to be! The worst of it is there's nothing we can do about it. Not at the moment. However, we have the rest of the day to call our own.' His smile was irresistible. 'And we have the rest of our lives.'

Sabina directed her eyes down to her plate. 'David,' she said, 'why didn't you tell me that the Somers had a daughter Shani who's at university in Helsinki?'

He said carelessly, 'Didn't I tell you?'

'You know you didn't.'

'Then it slipped my memory. So what?'

Sabina laid down her knife and fork, leaving the rest of the Karelian pastry; she had lost the taste for food. Nervously she put the glass of wine to her lips to fortify herself.

'Nothing really,' she replied, putting it down and

using her table napkin. 'The girl is so attractive that I'm surprised you didn't, that's all.'

He said teasingly, 'You've been looking at that picture of her, haven't you?'

'What picture?' Sabina echoed foolishly.

'The most recent one of Shani, on the piano there in the salon.' He gestured with his dark head towards the adjoining room from where they were sitting in the dining annexe.

Sabina had been aware of family portraits around the room but had not looked at them as yet. She had been enjoying the wonderful views over the lake from the tall windows too much to take stock of the more intimate details of the rooms. She could have kicked herself for being so remiss. But she was not of an inquisitive nature and the villa was only on lease, a fact which gave her reservations about people's property.

She swallowed on a dry throat and sipped a little more of the wine.

'Shall we be seeing Shani while we're here?' she asked.

A careless shrug. 'I doubt it.'

'Have you seen her since we came here to the villa?'

David pushed his empty plate away. He said abruptly, 'Look, what is this? An inquisition?'

Eila appeared at that moment with coffee on a tray containing two covered silver dishes.

'Nothing else for me, thanks,' he said. 'Just coffee.'

Eila's surprised expression included them both. Her mouth half opened before she spoke.

'No ice cream sponge? Only coffee?'

'Coffee for me too, please.' Sabina spoke with difficulty. She was beginning to realise that she should have told David about her meeting with Shani. There should be no secrets between husband and wife, especially those which made them unhappy. But David had been the one who had not been frank in the first place. Why should she be frank with him when he was not with her?

She was aware of Eila smiling down at them. 'I see you have enjoyed my Karelian pastry too much. You have no room for the ice cream sponge. I will forgive you,' she said, and led the way into the salon where she put the tray down on a low table between two comfortable chairs. 'There.' Her smile greeted them as they followed her into the salon. 'I will leave the sponge in case you change your minds.'

Her teasing had its effect. The atmosphere became less tense and David seated Sabina in one of the chairs before lowering his long length into the other.

The coffee was excellent, but Sabina hardly tasted it. David sat with his long legs outstretched drinking his slowly.

He said, 'What is this boat like that you went out in this morning? Comfortable? I was wondering whether you'd like to go out on the lake again this afternoon.'

'I don't mind,' she answered. 'The boat is in excellent condition.'

She knew that her voice lacked enthusiasm, but she could not for the life of her infuse any life into it. David obviously did not intend to discuss Shani unless he was going to do so on the lake. Actually, now that the initial shock had worn off, it was not the thought of him having an affair with the girl that hurt so much. It was the thought that he no longer loved the girl he had married. Maybe when the last operation on her face was over, and providing it was a success, he would quietly slip out of her life. And if it was not, would he still feel in honour bound to stay with her? Sabina loved him desperately, loved him enough to fight for him even to forgetting any affair with Shani. But she could not fight for a love which was not hers. She did not want a husband who did not love her, who had married her out of a sense of duty. The situation then would not only be humiliating, it would be intolerable.

Sabina could think of nothing more delightful than drifting along on the lake with David, two laughing, uncomplicated people. But they were not. David had lighted a cigar and the fragrant aroma coming from it wrapped his personality around her like shackles. He was near enough for her to run her fingers through his thick dark hair and tease him tenderly. There was a time when he used to tease her, but not any more. Her eyes wandered down the lean brown hand resting on the arm of his chair, and he turned his head to look at her in that same moment, his well-shaped head outlined against the light.

'Not too tired to go out again, are you?' he asked without expression. His dark face was unreadable and Sabina roused herself into a suitable response.

'Of course not. I wish you wouldn't treat me like an invalid.'

She had not intended to speak so roughly, but it was either that or scream. Why didn't she rave at him, make him tell her truth about Shani, about why he had married her? But the whole structure upon which her emotions were built had been undermined by the accident and the present healing stage would not withstand the whole shattering truth. She had to have more time.

'I'm sorry,' she whispered.

'Nothing to be sorry about.' He bent forward to the

low table to put out the lighted cigar. 'Shall we go?'

He did not touch her as they walked down to where she had left the boat, but he gave her his hand to steady her as she got in. It was warm and vibrant and caused Sabina to tremble a little. The attraction David had for her was strong and powerful. She doubted if it would ever wane even if he did disillusion her in the end.

He saw that she was comfortable among the cushions before he took up the oars. She closed her eyes as he rowed easily and strongly with rhythmic strokes. It was cool above the movement of the oars dipping in the water and her senses were sharpened by sweet sounds. Distant laughter echoed across the lake from the far side and she opened her eyes to see that David was some way out now following the line of the shore. The water was like glass, a mirror reflecting the surroundings around the edges. Everything seemed to be so unreal that Sabina dropped a hand to trail it in the water.

David looked strong and vital, his clear-cut features outlined in detail in the brilliant light.

'Nice here,' he said. 'There are several sheltered places where we can pull in if you like. Unless you want to go across the lake again?'

'It's fine here,' she said.

'Not sorry you came?'

'No. Are you?'

'Good lord, no. Not if you aren't.'

Her smile was wistful. 'Why should I be? I have you. The villa is fabulous. I like Eila and Leif and Max is on hand to do the last rites on my face.'

His dark eyes were suddenly keen. 'That's a funny way to describe your forthcoming restoration to beauty,' he mocked. 'Not still scared of the operation, are you?'

Sabina bit her lip and looked down at her fingers trailing in the water. Her voice was very low and she spoke without looking up.

'David, what if the operation isn't a success? Will you still want me?'

'Want you? We're married, aren't we?' He turned his head towards the shore and began to pull in towards it. 'We'd better take a walk along the shore.'

Sabina watched as he drew the boat nearer to the clump of trees overhanging the edge of the water. Then David was out and pulling the boat in. He helped her out and tied it up.

'Now,' he said, putting an arm around her and guiding her footsteps along by the water's edge, 'suppose we bring all those fears of yours out into the open. What's troubling you? Is it anything Max said this morning?'

'Of course not. Max is very understanding. I like him very much.'

'Not more than me, I hope?'

David had his hands on her shoulders and was turning her round slowly to face him. His finger was hard beneath her chin as he lifted her face to look deep into her eyes. Her breath was coming fast enough for it to choke her. She was beyond words as his eyes darkened into a searing need and his head shut out the light.

If she had thought that his kisses since their marriage had been lacking then the ones he gave her now more than made up for them. His mouth fastened on hers as though to draw her very soul through her lips. All she could do was to cling until he saw fit to release her. At first he was like a man driven by hunger. Sabina felt bruised and battered until he gradually became more gentle and she found the comfort she had been seeking since their marriage. She wanted the kisses to go on for ever so that she would never be alone again with her thoughts. The fear of it sent her own desires soaring to match his.

Sensing this, David laughed, the exultant laugh of a lover, scooped her up into his arms and strode with her to a grassy knoll beneath the lacy reflection of sheltering trees. There he laid her down and lowered his long length beside her. Sabina quivered as his hand moved caressingly over her breast and he began to kiss her again in slow, long-drawn-out kisses. The plane overhead came out of nowhere, went in a flash but was followed by a shattering sound as it broke the sound barrier. Sabina was suddenly the victim of her own violence. Within seconds she had pushed him out of the way, was on her feet and running on the wings of fear.

It was not only the shattering bang which had caused her flight, she was against David making love to her until she was sure that he loved her. It was impossible for her to give herself until she knew the truth of why he had married her. She ran like a hunted fawn, but his long legs finally caught up with her.

'Sabina, my poor sweet,' he murmured in her hair as he drew her gently against him.

And Sabina, danger averted, crumpled against his broad chest in a flood of tears. Between gasping for breath and weeping she was mentally and physically exhausted. Her tears had nothing to do with the unexpected breaking of the sound barrier by the plane which had only served to open the floodgates of her inner distress.

Soothing and caressing her, David held her close until she gradually grew quiet, then he gave her his hand-kerchief.

'Better now?' he asked.

She blew her nose and gave a last dab at her tear-drenched eyes.

'Sorry,' she said weakly. 'I'm afraid the front of your shirt is damp.'

'That's what I like about you, my sweet. Always thinking of others before yourself,' he commended her with genuine feeling. 'You wouldn't let anything bother you without telling me, would you?'

Huskily she said, 'I could ask you the same question.'

He laughed at her frankness. 'Darling, I want frankness between us at all times. But most of all I want to look after you. It's a little weakness I have. And after all, I am your husband, my sweet.'

Sabina stared up at him, poignantly aware of her love. She loved him more than anything else in the world. And David, concerned and kind, was returning his handkerchief to his pocket after giving her a poser which she had no idea how to answer.

She could only say, 'I'm not behaving very well, am I?'

She trembled and he placed a comforting arm around her. 'Forget it. Let's go back to the villa for a cup of tea. It's good for shock and you must be feeling dehydrated after all that weeping.'

He drew her against him and they walked back to where he had moored the boat. Having seated her comfortably he picked up the oars and pulled strongly to send the craft skimming through the water. Sabina sat without lifting her eyelashes still moist from her tears. Weeping had not marred her attractiveness. Her hair was spun gold where the sun touched it, the bright sunlight outlined the enchanting curves of her head, her temples, the line down to her chin where a curtain of hair concealed the scar on her cheek. She looked young, sweet, and untouched, and if David was puzzled by her behaviour, he was not without a slight compunction at the way he had handled her when she was not ready.

He said, 'What about having tea on the lawn? I'll go to the kitchen for it while you go to freshen up. That all right?'

Sabina nodded without looking up and at last they reached the villa. While David moored the boat she went quickly upstairs. On the way she was stopped halfway upstairs by the shrill ringing of the telephone below her in the hall. David entered the villa at that moment and strode across the room to pick up the receiver.

When she reached her room her mind was again riddled with doubt about him. Could it have been Shani telephoning him? Sensibly she told herself sternly to stop meeting trouble halfway and set about washing her tear-stained face in cool clear water. She combed her hair, applied a little make-up, adding a whisper of blue on her swollen lids, then put on a sun-dress of a yellow sunflower design on a white background.

David was putting the tray down on to the canopied table on the lawn when she strolled out into the sunshine. The scene with the sparkling lake in the background was inviting and David looked arrogantly handsome with the sun shining on his dark head. Ignominiously, her legs shaking under her, and accepting the chair he pulled out for her, Sabina sank into it, longing for his nearness, yet half afraid, as before, of what could happen.

His smile at her was appraising as he handed her a cup of tea.

'I like the sun-dress,' he said with a twinkle. 'Try one of these sandwiches. They look delicious.'

Sabina looked down at the open sandwiches topped

with savoury and sweet fillings, and took one. She did not feel in the least like eating, but at least it was something to do.

David was on his lounger drinking his tea and staring out across the sparkling water. The sun was on his strong profile, his firm brown throat in the open-necked sports shirt, and it made her feel weak just to look at him. The sandwich was delicious and she munched in silence. Then David lazily turned a head and drawled, 'How do you feel about going out this evening?'

'You mean with you?'

'I mean dining out. Urfo Mikkola has invited us to dine at his home with his sister Kirsty.'

'You mean just the two of them. No one else?'

'That's right. I know how you feel about crowds at the present moment. He telephoned just now. It appears his sister works at a hospital in Helsinki and comes home once a month to spend the day with him.'

David's tone and the cool competence of his manner was meant to put her at her ease. He knew what he was doing, Sabina told herself, knew and understood the complex situation better than she did, and she was about to refuse when curiosity got the better of her. After all, facing two people did not present a problem. Urfo could already know about her scarred face. And she was curious about Kirsty because she had once been engaged to Max Hiltunsen.

She finished her sandwich and licked the tips of her fingers daintily.

'Did you know that Max was once engaged to Urfo's sister?' she asked.

'No I didn't. Does that mean you will go?'

She laughed. 'You mean you know I will because I'm curious to see Max's ex-girl-friend?'

'I'm glad you accept.' He smiled at her, with no hint of mockery. 'You know something—I'm beginning to miss Sabina Farne. I much prefer her to the present Sabina Savelon.'

Sabina felt a sense of guilt, although his voice was more gentle than reproachful. 'I'm sorry,' she said. 'It's all the worry of the operation on my face. Oh, David, if anything goes wrong I don't think I shall be able to bear it.'

'Nothing is going to go wrong,' he asserted. 'So stop worrying about it. Tell yourself you're going to enjoy your evening out and you will. And never shrink from trouble. Always stand up to it and you'll find it isn't as bad as you thought.'

His voice was deep and reassuring, the hand he placed over her quivering one as he reached across the table was warm and comforting. Her fingers curled around his and she was sorely tempted to ask him about Shani. But he had already witnessed a surfeit of tears, more than enough for one day. So the moment passed.

CHAPTER THREE

SABINA found Urfo Mikkola and his sister Kirsty very likeable. He was the more delicate-looking of the two, with pale grey eyes enlivened by dark-rimmed spectacles and blond hair. Against his five foot six or so Kirsty was a little taller and darker in colouring. Her hair and eyes were dark brown, her figure trim and neat, and she looked lithe and strong. For all their shyness brother and sister showed a lively interest in their guests.

Sabina and David had driven to the charming villa by car. Urfo offered Sabina his hand and David turned to Kirsty. She heard David say something conventional to Kirsty, then brother and sister were apparently taken with his charm and everyone appeared to relax.

Much to Sabina's relief the evening began without the slightest hint of strain one expects upon meeting strangers. David was soon deep in conversation with Urfo, leaving Sabina to make the acquaintance of Kirsty over the aperitif they had before their meal.

Kirsty said, 'I have been looking forward to meeting you. What do you think of our country, Mrs Savelon?'

Whether by accident or design her brown eyes had not once wandered to the scar on Sabina's cheek, a fact which warmed Sabina to her.

'I like it very much. It's so naturally beautiful.'

Kirsty's brown eyes twinkled. 'When one is on one's honeymoon any country is heaven, is it not? I trust you have recovered from your accident?'

'All except the scar.' Sabina found that she could refer to it without embarrassment with Kirsty. 'I need a final operation.'

Kirsty regarded it dispassionately. 'You are fortunate in being so pretty one hardly notices it. I would look revolting with a scar like that.'

Sabina said stoutly, 'No, you wouldn't. I bet you would be braver than I am about it. I hate it and I can't wait for the time when it will be operated on. Max has promised to do it for me soon.'

Kirsty's colour rose to her face. 'Max? You mean Max Hiltunsen?'

'Yes. I don't know what I would have done without him. You know him, of course, since he's practically your neighbour?'

'Yes. We have known each other since children.' Kirsty found her drink interesting and gazed down into it. 'Have you seen Helsinki yet, Mrs Savelon?'

'No. I'm looking forward to seeing it with David.'

Sabina graciously accepted the sudden change in the conversation with the feeling that Kirsty did not want to discuss Max Hiltunsen now or at any time. What had happened between them, the breaking off of their engagement, must have been fairly conclusive. How old was Kirsty? Nearing thirty? An age when some women set their heart on becoming independent in a career. What a waste, since she was obviously excellent mother material, with her sweet disposition and placid manner. Sabina could imagine the patients in her care at the hospital being very fond of her.

She listened while Kirsty advised her on things to see, the lakes, of which there were many, the pine forests, and the midnight sun with its strange mysterious glow lasting from the end of May until late July. As the meal progressed Sabina noted that Kirsty and her brother were very fond of each other, also that Urfo was not as nondescript as he appeared to be. He was clever in his work as an engineer and David listened to him intently with obvious admiration for his views on the project they were engaged in.

'I do not know why Urfo does not seek some nice woman to share his life,' Kirsty said during a lull in the conversation.

Urfo laughed at the absurdity of such a suggestion. 'Why should I contemplate marriage when I have a full life in my career? I am happy.'

'There, you see,' Kirsty cried in good humour. 'What can you do with a brother like that? I have a weekend off from the hospital, but I do not see him. I don't know why I bother to come home. Now if you had a wife, Urfo, we could be good friends and company for each other.'

Kirsty's eyes were twinkling in a way that lighted up her whole face and made her very attractive. Idiotically Sabina wished that Max Hiltunsen could see her now.

David said lazily, 'If it's a companion you want why not go out with Sabina on the days that I'm locked in combat with my colleagues? I'm sure she'll be delighted to go out with you.'

'Ah, that is a good suggestion, but surely you do not want a third person during your honeymoon?' Kirsty answered delicately.

'We have an understanding, Kirsty,' Sabina cut in hastily. 'As David suggests, I'd be delighted to go out with you on the days when he's otherwise engaged.'

The evening came to an end on a reluctant note. Sabina had enjoyed it immensely and told Kirsty so when they parted. Kirsty kissed her.

'I will call for you tomorrow in my car and we will have a good day. I am so happy to have met you, and David,' she said warmly.

For a while David drove in silence. Before them the road unwound in a strange light which sprayed the lake and the woods with an unearthly beauty. The midnight sun, streaming through the trees, turned night into day.

'What a strange and wonderful light,' Sabina murmured with her head against David's shoulder. 'It's so beautiful it's almost uncanny.'

They had reached the villa and he shut off the engine to gaze down into her glowing face.

'Let's go for a short stroll before bed,' he said.

She laughed up into his face. 'It's been an enchanting evening.'

'You're an enchanting person, Mrs Savelon.'

He bent his head and kissed her. His lips were hard upon hers and his arms enfolded her in a steely strength. Sabina melted. Nothing and no one existed for her but David, her husband. Then he let her go.

'Come on,' he urged. 'I'll put the car away later.'

The midnight sun streaming across the lake turned the surface into a living thing of molten metal. On the far side of the lake boats were out and laughter rippled on the warm night air. Sabina felt a strange breathlessness as David sought her hand to clasp it lightly in strong fingers. For the time being all tension had gone and life was considerably simplified. David, she thought, had a flair amounting to genius for dealing with difficult situations. He was so receptive to new ideas, listened rather than argued, and lazily enjoyed himself. He had already accepted the slower tempo of life, new food, new friends and the cordial hospitality.

But for her it was not so easy. At the moment his close

handclasp was sending vibrations through her like an electric current. They reminded her that despite his good grooming he was very much a primitive man underneath with all a man's needs. And they were still almost strangers. They had progressed no further than being good friends with warm, often passionate kisses to cement their unity. Sometimes in a few swift glances David had touched her heart, had hinted at a very different and exciting world beyond the one she knew. He had made her feel since meeting him that her life hitherto had retained a dream-like quality about it rather like the strange light of the midnight sun that picked out the tanned arrogance of his profile as he looked across the lake.

'Well, Mrs Savelon, I'm sure you'll agree that this is a perfect setting for a honeymoon.'

They had stopped near the water's edge and he was turning her around slowly to face him. Sabina saw his well-cut lips quirk tenderly into a smile as he drew her into his arms.

'This is what I've been waiting for all day,' he whispered as he bent his head. Ardent moments passed, ecstatic moments as she soared to a pinnacle of joy. His kisses deepened. He was all fire and laughter. His dark eyes looked black when, for a moment, he lifted his head to gaze silently upon the frank enchantment of her face.

Sabina felt the spell of his magnetism, finding him as wonderful as on the first day they had met with the treasures of the antique shop bringing heaven very near. The scar on her face had magnified in importance, cutting through the centre of her life like an abyss. On one side stood a pale Sabina, apprehensive and afraid. On the other, the former warm-hearted and loving girl, grateful for the chance of loving her dear, wonderful

David. As he held her in his arms with his lips cleaving to hers she could feel his hands, strong, yet infinitely, marvellously gentle on her body. Caressing every curve and line, he eventually cupped her small pointed breast in beloved fingers. His voice had been quiet and steady, but now it thickened as he whispered against her lips all the endearments that a bride loves to hear.

In his arms Sabina ceased to think of Shani and her hysterical outburst. Rather incoherently she found herself thinking, this is love. This is what marriage means. Love culminating in a grand passion but love nevertheless. Later she would lose some of her own identity by becoming part of David. She would be his. But would he be hers? She refused to listen to the nagging doubt and matched her passion with his. Then, just as she was sure that every bone in her body would crack in his fierce hold, he buried his lips into her neck and muttered thickly, 'Let's go in.'

Feeling dazed but very happy, Sabina continued indoors while he put the car away. She drifted across the hall in the golden light of the sun streaming through tall windows, whirled around like a dancer with slender arms outstretched, and then embraced the carved wooden pillar of the staircase. For several moments she leaned a slightly feverish forehead against the cool wood before the shrill ringing of the telephone nearby startled her into reality. David was coming in through the door as she picked up the receiver.

'For you,' she said, then went blindly up the stairs. There was no mistaking Shani's voice asking for David. The silence of the night met her as she entered the room in all melancholy, and she shivered in spite of the sun lighting up the tall windows. Where did one go from here? Surely not back to the naïve and pliable idiot she had been in David's arms. She drifted over to the window and gazed out unseeingly on a scene almost as bright as day. Unreality engulfed her now of a different kind. Minutes ago the perfume of the night had been all around her, mingling with the wild glad beating of her heart, while David's voice had whispered to her with a new unsteady break in it. Even had she been more experienced, being flung from such emotional heights left her in no fit state to reason. And the shattering of her dreams within the last few minutes was beyond reason.

How long she stood there Sabina never knew. The sound of David's voice brought her back to reality. His hands were on her shoulders as he kissed her hair. Sabina held her breath. He was going to tell her about the telephone call, about Shani. Somehow she managed to speak lightly.

'Well, have you to go out again tomorrow or have we got the day together?'

'Tomorrow?' he echoed vaguely. 'Are you aware, my darling, that it's past midnight and already tomorrow? As a matter of fact I do have to go out tomorrow. An important conference which I can't wriggle out of. What made you ask?'

His lips were moving from her ear to the side of her neck and she felt her inside coiling up into a tight ball. So he was not going to say anything about the telephone call.

'The telephone call just now—surely that wasn't to tell you about the conference. Not at midnight?'

'Oh, that!' He laughed. 'Hardly. Even the most dedicated of secretaries are usually off duty at midnight. It was nothing important.'

'Then why did she call at this unearthly hour if it

wasn't? Surely it could have waited until morning?' She moved out of his arms. 'I forgot—it is morning, isn't it, and I'm tired.'

'Of course you are, my pet. I won't keep you long. Do you want any help with your zip?'

Sabina backed a step, her hand already lifted to take down the zip at the back of her dress.

'I can manage, thanks,' she said. He had reached the door of his dressing room before she plucked up enough courage to say, 'I'll say goodnight as I won't be seeing you until morning.'

David had stopped dead with his hand on the door of his dressing room, and during the heavy silence which followed he neither turned nor did he speak. He spoke at last without expression.

'And why don't you want me to come in to you? Don't you want me as your husband?'

She turned to stare at his back, at the wide shoulders and lean tapering hips, and a lump caught in her throat. 'No, nothing like that.'

There was so much pain in her voice that she could not go on. She twisted her hands and her mouth trembled too much to form further words.

'You mean it's beyond your powers to love me? You have nothing to give?'

'I've so much to give you, only . . . only . . .' again she faltered.

'Only what?' he said curtly.

'I want you to give me a little more time. Everything has happened so quickly. I'm—I'm so confused.' Sabina covered her face with her trembling hands. Then he was there gripping her wrists, forcing her hands away from her face.

'Two minutes ago you were returning my kisses as though you meant them,' he muttered between tight lips.

She cried piteously, 'I did mean them. Oh, please understand! I can't bear to hurt you. I don't mean you personally. I—I—have to get something straight in my mind.'

'You mean you don't want to go any further than the kissing stage,' he said bluntly.

Sabina was silent pondering his words, which he believed were more or less the truth. Then she drew a shuddering sigh.

'Couldn't we . . . wouldn't you agree to our being as we are for a short time?'

He dropped her hands as if he could not bear to touch them, and said roughly, 'Anything platonic between us is out. You should have chosen a man who loved you less tremendously, less demandingly than I do. Too bad that you've landed yourself with an insatiable husband. However, I want nothing that you won't give willingly. I could assert what are called my rights but, in my opinion, there are no such things as rights in marriage. Everything that happens between husband and wife must be given freely with love, not from a sense of duty. A marriage in which the partners think in terms of duty and rights is finished before it's begun.'

Her lips trembled. 'Perhaps, at the back of my mind, I've known all along that we married too soon after the accident.'

Harshly he replied, 'I'm beginning to think that, otherwise I wouldn't be standing here arguing with you like this. I'd take you, make you as much mine in body as you are mine by law. But I can't, and do you know why?' He took hold of her shoulders as though he would shake her. 'Because I don't want you that way. When you give yourself to me it will be because you want me, not by passion taking the upper hand. Heaven knows I'm no saint and I've no scruples on my part, but I have to see this thing done my way. I'll go along with you for the present. In the meantime keep out of my way as much as you can. I'm only human.'

He released her so abruptly that she staggered back against the bed and fell on it. When his door closed Sabina had never felt so lonely in her life. His reluctance to tell her about the telephone call from Shani could only mean one thing, that there was something going on between them. Turning over on her side, she cradled her head in her arm and wept silently and hopelessly.

CHAPTER FOUR

WHEN she awoke the following morning Sabina recalled the events of the previous night with mixed emotions. At first there was only anger because David had not been frank with her in the first place. Of Shani, she could not think beyond the sudden pain the girl had inflicted in her scorn at her scarred face. Shani was young enough to crave excitement and David was the type, good-looking, charming and dynamic enough to give her all the excitement she wanted.

Thinking it out calmly her first instinct was to leave him, since it was obvious that he did not love her. Her refusal to let him make love to her had only hurt his vanity. She might be the first girl who had refused his advances. That he had never sought to seduce her before they married did not mean a thing since he knew by now that she was not the kind to play around. Had she been so wrong about him, his consideration, his tenderness, the magical quality his strength of mind and body held for her? Could she leave him now and put his future prospects in jeopardy?

For there was his job to consider. He could easily lose the one big chance in his life to further his career if they were to break up now. The company who were considering him would naturally think that he was unstable if his wife left him on their honeymoon. And he was anything but that. After all, you do not give everything up, your hopes, your dreams, and all that makes life worth living at the drop of a hat. But could she be a true wife to a man who did not want her, a man who had married her out of a sense of duty? There was no sound of any movement from his dressing room, which could mean that she could have been awakened by the sound of his car leaving the villa. Her watch said nine o'clock. She had overslept. David, of course, would not oversleep. He might even have been up earlier than usual with no feeling of regret at the way things had turned out. It was possible that he was enjoying a sense of relief that she had found a way out of their marriage for both of them.

She was staring into space with the kind of numbness which follows a shattering experience when Eila entered with her breakfast.

'Good morning, Mrs Savelon,' she smiled. 'I trust you had a good night. Mr Savelon said you were sleeping when he left and he asked me to bring your breakfast at nine because you are going out for the day with a friend.'

Sabina had forgotten about Kirsty. 'Oh, goodness, yes,' she cried, pushing herself up in bed to receive the tray. The thought of having a new friend boosted her morale, for in her present predicament movement was essential.

Kirsty arrived at ten o'clock in her own car. She wore a sleeveless dress in brown linen enlivened by a choker necklace of white beads and white studs clipped to her ears. Her smooth skin was lightly tanned and her brown eyes looked hazel in the bright sunlight. There were auburn tints in her brown hair and she looked quite attractive.

'Not calling too early, am I?' she asked when Sabina tripped out of the villa to greet her. 'Your husband suggested ten o'clock, as you were late going to bed.'

'You mean David telephoned you this morning?' Sabina hid her surprise as she slid into the car.

'Yes. Didn't he tell you?'

Kirsty turned the car round to face the driveway, then continued on her way.

'I was asleep when he left,' Sabina said as offhandedly as she was able. 'I've brought my swimsuit in case I need it.'

'That's fine, because I've brought a picnic basket so we can lounge the day away.'

One of the joys of motoring in this strange and wonderful country, Sabina thought, was the panoramic view from a car driving along an open road which seemed to stretch into eternity. Kirsty gave the impression of meandering through the heart of lake country, across bridges stapling bright blue water, past farms and forests. A surfeit of laybys went by as they drove along the main highway. Some of them had folding tables and chairs in readiness along with wooden tables and benches.

Kirsty explained that to cut the risk of fire down to a minimum people were encouraged to use the picnic areas laid out for them. The hills were very low and the lakes shallow, which meant that they were easily warmed by the sun.

Sabina soon became familiar with the Finnish signs— *ravintola* for restaurant, *kalvila* for café and *baari* for bar. The lake they stopped at lay on the edge of a forest where the scented air was aromatic to the nostrils. Sabina breathed it in, deeply happy to see that the lake was deserted but for one small boat silhouetted against the blue sky.

The placid water was warm and welcoming and Sabina loved the caressing feeling as it closed soft as silk over her limbs. Kirsty was the stronger swimmer. Her biceps were hardened through being on her feet all day at the hospital and she was soon striking out with scarcely a ripple. But Sabina's long legs stood her in good stead and she swam out for some distance before turning back to the shore.

Later when they sat down near the water's edge to enjoy the excellent and ample picnic Kirsty had provided, Sabina thought smugly that she had the best of it with David sitting in on some conference. But the smugness did not last for long, for she ached for his presence. She wanted him completely, had known it from the day they had met.

They were lying stretched out and replete with their lunch when Kirsty asked casually, 'Did you know your husband long before you married him?'

'Six months. We met in an antique shop in London.'

'He is a very attractive man with lots of charm. I suppose he swept you off your feet?'

Kirsty's tone was free from rancour and Sabina smiled. 'You could say he knocked me off my feet. We collided later the same day in the street.'

'By accident or design?'

'By accident, I suppose. It was pouring heavens hard with rain and I wasn't looking where I was going.' A thought suddenly struck her. 'You don't mean to say that David ran into me on purpose?' She laughed, found the idea very pleasant, and laughed again.

Kirsty chuckled. 'Why shouldn't he? I bet he wasn't the first man to make advances to you.'

'Why should you say that?'

'Because you are so very attractive—and I don't mean in looks. You have a warm loving nature and it shows. I've never attracted men—I'm much too tall and clumsy. I have big hips which I camouflage by wearing straight skirts. I usually end up being a confidante of the male staff at the hospital. They tell me all their troubles.'

'Then you do attract men. Don't you see, you must, since they confide in you?'

Kirsty said dryly, 'Men confide in their doctor or their priest, but they never think of marrying them.'

Sabina laughed. 'Have you ever been in love, Kirsty? I keep calling you Kirsty and I hope you will call me Sabina. Will you, please? I'd like to think of you as my friend.'

'I was in love once, but never again,' Kirsty told her. 'If I marry it will be for companionship.'

Kirsty's voice had a bitter ring and Sabina said slowly, 'What happened?'

'He preferred someone else.'

'Oh, Kirsty, I am sorry. Are you sure, though? You know, you're a very attractive person, and when you laugh you kind of scintillate. Did he tell you, this man you loved, that he was in love with someone else?'

'Other people kept telling me about seeing him with her and when I caught them together, he did not deny it.'

'And you didn't ask him for an explanation?'

Kirsty shrugged. 'No. I refused to see him again. A relative of his was taken ill at the time and he had to give all his spare time to her. I saw him with this other girl from time to time afterwards. They are not together now, but I think they have an understanding.'

'Did the girl tell you that?' Sabina asked thoughtfully.

'Yes. She also told me that they were having an affair.'

'And you believed her? Didn't it occur to you that she might not have been speaking the truth?'

'No.' Kirsty was adamant. 'You see, she was younger

and much prettier than I am, the kind that men go for. I could understand him in a way choosing her. What amazed me was him choosing me in the first place.'

Sabina said dryly, 'He probably fell in love with you.'

'Well, it was soon over, wasn't it?'

'The question is did you love him?'

'I'd rather not talk about it. It's over and done with. However did we get on this subject anyway?'

'You brought it up,' Sabina said forcefully. 'It seems to me that you're so full of your own imagined shortcomings you can't see straight, much less recognise love when it comes. I hope you won't take offence at my plain speaking, but I think you need it, Kirsty.'

Kirsty gave an unhappy sigh. 'It has come too late in my case. I am sorry I told you about it.'

Sabina said hastily, 'Please don't say that. You've helped me a lot because I've been feeling like you did and wondering why David married me, scar and all. Now I know that I can never let him go without a fight.'

'Let him go?' Kirsty gave a startled glance. 'Are you not happy, then?'

'Let's say I shan't be happy until the scar on my face is removed. It bothers me very much.'

'I understand. But you have nothing to worry about. I envy you your David. You are lucky, and I am sure you will be very happy if you will only be patient.'

Sabina folded her arms behind her head and gazed up into the leafy protection of trees overhead. She wondered what David was doing at that moment, decided that guessing was futile, and closed her eyes.

They lay and dozed for most of the afternoon, then after a last dip in the lake, Kirsty suggested driving to a small town about ten minutes away to round off their day.

The town was not very big, but the shops were interesting to Sabina, who spent some time looking at the women's fashions in one particular store. She thought the dresses, lightweight, because of the warmth in the dwellings, were rather bright in colour, but the women looked very attractive in them. They were mostly on the tall side and carried themselves well.

She bought two pairs of reindeer house slippers for David and herself, some pretty place mats with views of Finland on them and a matching set of table napkins. Kirsty was after new socks for Urfo when they encountered a tall, fair, hatless man emerging from the gents' outfitters shop.

Max Hiltunsen divided his charming smile between them. 'I knew something nice was going to happen to me today,' he said. 'Enjoying some shopping, Sabina? You are quite a stranger, Kirsty.'

It was Kirsty who answered. 'We are in a hurry, Max, so if you will excuse us,' she said frigidly.

His bow was one of politeness and Sabina did not quite know what to do. It was evident that Kirsty did not want to talk to him. But he was big and standing directly in their path. Maybe he was being deliberately obtuse, for he was so much at ease, so much in command of the situation that Sabina said desperately, 'Hello, Max. I don't suppose you've seen anything of David by any chance? He went to a conference this morning.'

'No. You are not looking for him, are you?'

'No. Kirsty and I are out for the day.' Sabina paused uncertainly as Kirsty walked past Max and made her way into the shop. 'She's a charming person and I'm having a delightful time.'

'Then I must not intrude. Kirsty, no doubt, has everything planned for your enjoyment. I shall see you again soon, I trust when you dine with us.'

He was smiling down at her, looking opulent and very attractive in a beautifully cut city-going suit in pale grey. There was no doubt about it. He was a very attractive man and Sabina wondered fleetingly how deep his feelings went regarding Kirsty, since he was once engaged to her. Was he as unhappy about it as Kirsty appeared to be, and why had he let her go so easily? Surely that proved how shallow his feelings for her were. Sabina could not make it out, but she did not miss the faint shadow in his fine eyes as he took her hand.

Perhaps she was acting too hastily, but Sabina felt that she had to make up to him for Kirsty's behaviour.

'We could come for dinner this evening, David and I. If that would be all right,' she said warmly.

He gave her the kind of smile warm enough to touch any woman's heart.

'Delightful,' he replied. 'Shall we say eight o'clock?'

The next moment he had gone. When she joined Kirsty the shop assistant was showing her some socks in pure wool. Sabina fingered them and thought about David. She would have loved to have bought him some in the softer colour shades, but she knew so little about his likes and dislikes, it was difficult.

Kirsty was putting her purchases in her bag and they were leaving the shop when Sabina said, 'I wonder what Max bought.'

A brief silence. Then Kirsty said with a certain amount of restraint, 'You like him? What woman does not?'

Sabina was wary. 'You don't, Kirsty. You wouldn't have been so rude to him just now if you did.'

Kirsty went pale around her small nostrils, and said

coldly, 'I do not wish to discuss Max Hiltunsen now or at any other time. I am sorry, Sabina, that is all I have to say.'

Sabina was immediately contrite. 'I'm sorry, I didn't mean to offend. But you are two nice people and I thought that no one should be as unhappy as you appear to be over something which a little explaining could alter.'

'Explaining?'

The look of horror in Kirsty's brown eyes at the very idea panicked her somewhat and she said awkwardly, 'Oh, dear, I seem to have put my foot in it. I'm truly sorry, Kirsty. The last thing I want is to upset you. Am I forgiven?'

Kirsty smiled. 'Of course. Shall we take some refreshment? What about the open-air restaurant by the lake on our way back?'

The restaurant overlooking the lake was a mellowed wooden building bright with flowers with a front lawn covered with tables and chairs. A few of the tables were occupied with tanned, athletic young people who were on holiday. They chose a table on the edge of the water and ordered an iced drink with refreshments. The atmosphere between them lightened as they blissfully quenched their thirst and nibbled pastries strange to Sabina but delicious. If anything, she thought, the incident of Max had brought Kirsty and herself closer.

She was sorry when their outing drew to a close and Kirsty dropped her off at the villa, promising to let her know when they could arrange another meeting. David had not returned when Sabina went in search of Eila to tell her that they would be dining out that evening. Eila was pleased since, in their absence, she and Leif would be free to pay a visit to her mother who lived in a cottage not far away from the villa.

Sabina showered and changed into one of her evening dresses in delicate eggshell blue muslin and lace. The dainty edge of the full long skirt was pintucked and the matching sandals were in broderie anglaise. Her hair felt like golden silk as she brushed it, a sure sign that her health was improving and that the time was drawing near when Max would find her fit enough for further treatment on her face. The thought cheered her somewhat but did nothing to dispel the ordeal of waiting for David.

How would he greet her after last night? She had never seen him so angry and he had not relented before leaving that morning because he had not left any written message even to say when he would be back. Well, if he did not come she would go to dine with Max alone, and leave a note to say where she had gone.

He came striding in the room as she trod into the pretty sandals. Her heart lurched as he closed the door and took his time eyeing her from head to toe. She stood silent and palpitating in a dress which looked as though it had been untouched by human hand. Its fragile beauty enhanced her smooth skin tanned to a light gold, the super-shiny blonde hair and huge expressive eyes fringed with thick dark lashes.

For a moment a gleam came into the dark inscrutable eyes before David narrowed them into something cold as the snows.

'Going places?' he queried on an uplifted brow. 'Or is it for me?'

Sabina swallowed painfully and lifted a militant chin to show the enchanting curve of her slender neck and jaw.

But her smile, half sweet, half wistful, did not touch him.

'We're dining with Max—I met him today when I was out with Kirsty. I hope you haven't made other arrangements.'

David shrugged. 'What time are we expected?'

He sounded tired and fed up, and her heart went out to him. 'Eight o'clock.' She offered the reindeer slippers, 'I bought these for you this afternoon.'

But he made no attempt to accept them. 'What is it?' he asked cynically. 'A bribe to be on my best behaviour? You're asking a lot, looking as you do at this moment.' His voice was on ice as he surveyed her quivering form. 'With your hair shimmering like gold, your eyes deep blue pools that a man can drown in, you represent an oasis to a starving man, and I'm only human like the rest.'

He came nearer and Sabina felt the pull of his magnetism. Another moment and she would have been in his arms—but she had her pride. She pulled herself together and resorted to anger. It was her only weapon against him.

'For goodness' sake, can't I buy you a present without receiving insults?' she cried. 'Here, take your present. As for last night, I'm sorry, truly I am. You must make allowances.'

Inexorably, he said, 'Such as?'

Sabina had thrust the present at him and he held it indifferently in strong brown hands.

'Go on,' he scoffed, 'what allowances? That you don't love me?'

Had he been more approachable, even unbent a little from his steely attitude, she would have flung herself into his arms. But his mouth had taken on a hard cruel slant.

She said tremulously, 'I love you. I need time.'

'You don't love me. All the time in the world would make no difference to you. Love should be spontaneous, a joyous thing. All this talk about allowances, time—you make me sick! I told you last night that duty and rights have nothing to do with a happy marriage. If you haven't learned that by now you never will.'

'But, David . . .' she cried as he strode to his dressing room. He did not turn, and she sank down into the nearest chair as he closed his door behind him.

When he came out again in evening dress she was standing by the window waiting for him.

He said, 'Have you told Eila that we're dining out?'

She nodded woodenly. They were outside the villa when he spoke again.

'Do you want to go across the lake or by car?' he asked evenly.

Sabina bit her lip, uncertain what to say, and David looked dispassionately at the pretty mohair stole draped around her slim shoulders.

'The air will be cooler on the water, but your wrap seems adequate, so what about taking the boat? Makes a change from breathing in car fumes—besides, it's appropriate to the occasion.' He slanted her a sardonic glance and added, 'Our honeymoon.'

He looked big and strong and uncaring, almost insolent, and Sabina hated this side of him. Unfortunately there was nothing to be done about it since nothing she might say would put them on the frank and happy footing they had enjoyed before the wedding. David was so convinced that she did not love him—or was it a game he was playing? Did he want things the way they were? Sabina felt small, alone and utterly miserable.

The boat lay moored and ready with the added

cushions left, no doubt, by Leif earlier on for them to use, since crossing the lake was not only the shortest way but by far the nicest. David had lifted a hand to her elbow as they reached the lake and the sudden whirring noise above her head happened simultaneously. The bird, disturbed by their quiet approach, flew out of the trees near by and swooped very close to her head. Startled, she gripped David's arm and crouched against his chest.

She was thoroughly unnerved and stood there trembling and gripping him fiercely. Her skin felt cold and clammy and made her shiver, yet she was hot inside.

'It's all right,' he assured her. 'It was only a bird.'

His arms were warm around her, his breath warm on her hair. Weak tears fought to escape beneath her eyelids and she valiantly kept them back. She forced herself to stiffen against his hold, knowing that every moment was battering down her defences.

'I'm sorry.' Her voice was muffled against his chest and she felt his arms tightened around her.

He said reassuringly, 'Not to worry. These things do happen. Would you rather go by car?'

She shook her head. His arms were making it difficult for her to breathe. Her heart laboured on in a sharp exquisite pain followed by a wave of tenderness. Was it wrong to hold back when she loved him so much? With love went trust, so why was she afraid for her own happiness? She had to trust him, she had to love him. Oh, David, her heart cried, I'll give you everything you want of me.

Still trembling a little, she drew back. Pale as the blossoms blown by the breeze around them, she managed a smile.

'I'm all right now.'

'Sure?' he asked, his dark intent face very near.

'Yes, thank you.'

'Here we go, then. Mustn't wet your lovely dress.'

He scooped her up into his arms and placed her gently into the boat, and placed the cushions around her. It was going to be very hard to convince him of her love, but she would do so when they returned to the villa. Meanwhile she would silently adore him, with the hope that her love would get through to him in the end.

She was aware that he looked intensely strong and lean as he rowed effortlessly. His eyes beneath the straight dark brows, so dark that one could lose oneself in their blackness—if only he would look at her as he once did, intently, with all the tender regard of a man in love. They had almost reached the far side of the lake when he asked how she was feeling. The colour stole back in her cheeks, staining them to wild rose. Her lips curved into a smile.

'Fine,' she answered. 'It's so beautiful here on the water with that incredible sun shining as if it was day instead of evening. Have you met Max Hiltunsen's mother?'

David was turning his head and moving the boat in to land. 'No. I believe she was seriously ill a year ago— heart complaint. She was a singer.'

'Sounds interesting. That would be about the time that Max and Kirsty broke their engagement—I'm sure of it. Kirsty said there was some trouble for Max at the time. Perhaps that was why he and Kirsty had no time to sort out their differences.'

'Now look here,' David leaned forward as the boat drifted in, 'I don't hold with interfering in other people's lives, so don't you start anything.'

Before Sabina could reply he was out of the boat and

giving her a hand. Then Max was there, greeting them cordially.

'Mother cannot wait to meet you,' he told them as he walked in between them to the house where a woman waited to greet them.

Anna Hiltunsen had golden hair and hazel eyes. She was a well-preserved woman whose figure was still slim and youthful. Her dress, geranium crêpe trimmed with black beads, was chic and obviously a model gown. When Max introduced them she proffered a small beringed hand to Sabina.

'Max has told me so much about you that I could not wait to meet you. And your hair is as beautiful as he said it was—so golden!' She sighed. 'My hair was as pretty years ago. But I am getting old and it is no longer as beautiful as it was.'

Sabina looked soberly at the thick braids of silken golden hair coiled around the small head. Anna Hiltunsen looked around thirty-five, but she must be years older to have a son as old as Max. Her hair had scarcely begun to fade and her complexion was clear and youthful. First impressions told Sabina that here was a woman who put herself first on every occasion, a woman who through sheer vanity refused to allow herself to grow old. Having a son as good-looking and charming as Max helped to keep her young, since he probably accompanied her sometimes on their social rounds. Normally Sabina would not have harboured such thoughts, but as she met those hazel eyes she had a notion that the woman was jealous of her youth.

It was absurd really, but she could imagine how jealous Anna had been of Kirsty, and how easy it had been for her to make the girl think she was plainer than she really was. No one was going to have her son if she could help it!

The house was charming, with an open-plan décor. The huge picture windows gave a double-glazed panoramic view of the lake. The furniture was modern, and interpreted in a dashing, stylish design. Cushions, like the window drapes, were smart, dramatic to the eyes, like the spiral staircase and the giant brass-hooded fireplace.

Anna drifted through it all reliving her past glamorous life. Until her illness the previous year she had led a very active life with her singing engagements. Now there were no more public appearances, but she amused her guests sometimes with Max accompanying her at the piano.

Anna had wanted her son to become a concert pianist, although he had the ambition to be a doctor. His father, a local G.P., had encouraged him.

'My husband was not ambitious,' said Anna dispassionately. 'He died at the age of fifty through working night and day in a large sparsely populated area.'

'But why a plastic surgeon, Max?' David asked.

Anna waved a hand sparkling with rings. 'Did you not know that my son is soft-hearted? He was working in a large London hospital and he was so appalled at the terrible injuries caused through road accidents that he decided to specialise in plastic surgery.'

David grinned. 'Good for you, Max. The important thing is to do the job you want to do. Your heart isn't in it otherwise.'

Anna put her hands together in a dainty theatrical gesture. 'You, David, would have been a success in whatever you set out to do, I am sure. You and Mrs Savelon are a beautiful couple. So sad about the scar, but Max will put it right. I have a very clever son.'

Sabina could have said that Max had a clever mother, if a heartless one where his happiness was concerned. Nevertheless she enjoyed her evening. Anna was fine taken in small doses, and David found her amusing.

For a while David rowed in silence. The hour was late, for Anna had sung several of her songs for them with Max at the piano. In the end he had struck up with one or two popular songs from light operas in which they had all joined. All around them the lake shimmered in the glow of the midnight sun. Sabina sat demure and silent with her hands clasped in her lap as though in prayer. Their evening was over, but something much more important lay ahead.

So she sat, ever conscious of David's nearness, of the words he had said, that there were no rights in marriage, only love. He did not believe now that she loved him, so she had got to convince him that she did. Her heart gave a lurch at the thought that this was the night of all nights, for her at least. What a pity David had not taken her into his arms when she had repulsed him. He would have seen that she had been fighting against her love for him. Earlier that evening he had sat with a careless arm around her shoulders, joining in the songs with his deep baritone voice as though the two of them were as much in harmony in their private life as they were in song.

Anna had been enchanted with his voice. 'You and I will have to sing duets together the next time you come,' she cried enthusiastically.

It had struck Sabina then that David's good looks were shown to an advantage against Anna's fairness. Like her own. He was magnificently made, with the kind of face and body calculated to attract most women. But then Max was attractive in a different way. Where David's lovemaking would be arrogantly tender, Max Hiltunsen's would be just tender.

Life with David, Sabina was discovering, would not be easy all the time. But it would never cease to be exciting: she had known that from the moment their eyes had met at their first meeting. Every moment since then she had sensed a strange feeling of some part of her belonging to him by right. By right of love, of course. That was what he had taught her. Never before and never again would any man kindle the flame in her that David did.

She said, 'Did you enjoy the evening? I suppose we shall be seeing them again. You didn't appear to be very enthusiastic about going.'

His smile was enigmatic. 'I had my reasons, but I enjoyed it all right. And you?'

'I enjoyed it too.' Sabina looked dreamily over the water to the glow of the sun in the heavens. 'Isn't this a lovely way to travel? The rest of the world seems a million miles away.'

'It usually does on one's honeymoon,' he said sardonically, and smiled mockingly at the embarrassed expression on her face. His dark eyes narrowed into an expression which made her heart jolt as they slid lazily over her face and figure.

'From the tip of your golden head to your small dainty feet, you look transparent and fragile. It was a mistake to bring you across by boat. You'll interfere with my sleep far too much tonight.'

'You'll sleep all right,' she answered in the same teasing vein.

And he would, in her arms. To have him close, to hold

him to her, that was how she would convince him that she loved him. She had to.

Either that or face an impossible marriage. Sabina glanced at him quickly, then turned her eyes away to look down on the water. She locked her hands in her lap to prevent them from trembling. Perhaps her nervousness transmitted itself to David, because there was a tantalising inflection in the deep masculine voice when he leaned towards her over the oars with the sun highlighting his compelling good looks.

'Are you sure of that, Sabina?' he asked softly, dangerously.

A pulse beat in the base of her throat, but she managed to answer without much expression.

'You usually do what you want to do.'

He stared at her until she felt like screaming. 'Not always.' His smile was a little crooked. 'Am I to accept that as a challenge?'

Sabina hesitated. He was back in his dark insolent mood, a mood against which she was helpless. A sudden impulse to tell him about her hopes and fears, to pour out all her troubled mind against his wide chest, was almost too much to curb. But the habit of shyness, the dread of losing what little she had of him, withheld her. So she decided to keep it light by answering in the same vein.

'You're in a curious mood. I would have thought our evening out would have filled you full of blissful content, replete with good food and good music.'

He laughed mockingly. 'If music be the food of love, play on,' he jeered. 'A very minor part of a honeymoon, wouldn't you say? But then you're too frightened to let it go any further, aren't you?'

Sabina did not answer. He said no more and pulled

strongly for the shore. As the boat grounded, he was on the ground and lifting her out. She breathed in deeply, taken aback by the swift action, and released her breath when he set her on her feet. Uncertain what to do, she made her way towards the villa while David tied up the boat. It was then she saw the slight figure running to meet them.

'Hi there! I thought you were never coming!'

Sabina could not at once take in the details of Shani Somers' appearance. She could only stand and stare as the girl drew nearer. Then slowly the evening patio pyjama outfit she was wearing gradually took shape. Above it she looked insolently at Sabina as lips scarlet as the outfit she wore curled slightly.

'I understood David would be at home this evening. We met this afternoon, didn't he tell you?' she said, pushing back the dark hair with a slender armful of bangles.

'No.'

'How very strange!'

'I don't think so.' Sabina managed a smile. 'We had a dinner engagement. Anyway, whatever are you doing here at this hour?'

Shani lifted her thin shoulders. 'Really, David has let me down, hasn't he? Surely he told you that I might possibly be staying here for a few days? You see . . .'

No more explanations were forthcoming, as David joined them.

'Hello, Shani,' he said easily. 'My wife Sabina. Shall we go indoors?'

Sabina shrank inwardly from the careless arm David dropped around her shoulders. This was awful, as awful as her first meeting with the girl. Surely he would not invite her to stay? It might be Shani's home, but they were leasing the villa for their honeymoon and a third person was unthinkable when it was a little menace like her.

Meanwhile the little menace was talking ingratiatingly to David, walking between them with an arm around both.

'David, darling,' she cooed, 'you haven't told Sabina anything about me.' The pause was deliberate as she passed an oblique glance in Sabina's direction. 'Consequently I feel like a trespasser. Poor little me, gate-crashing on your honeymoon!'

Sabina felt like telling her that the remedy lay in her own hands. She had only to do the decent thing by leaving them in peace. But it was clear that Shani was going to do no such thing as they reached the villa.

By now Sabina had endured more than enough. Feeling slightly sick, she said, 'This is hardly the time to begin explanations about something which I know nothing about. So if you will excuse me I'll say goodnight.'

With a dignity that sat well on her slender shoulders, she went upstairs to her room. She felt absolutely numb. It was a numbness that followed shock and she dreaded the moment it wore off to lay bare the pain beneath. Was it Elizabeth Browning who said that a dropped star makes bitter waters? Well, her star had dropped, the star on which she had hung all her dreams, and the waters were bitter indeed.

CHAPTER FIVE

'I do not like it, Mrs Savelon. I look upon Shani's presence here as an intrusion on your privacy.'

Eila had brought Sabina's early morning drink and she placed the tray in front of her on the bed. Her usually pleasant smile was replaced by a grim look. She was upset.

'Mr and Mrs Somers would be very angry with Shani if they knew about it. Mr Savelon is being very nice about it, but it is my opinion that she should be sent away before . . .'

Eila stopped short, blushed furiously and straightened her back on an awkward silence.

'Go on and finish what you were going to say,' Sabina said wearily. 'You mean before she causes trouble. You know, of course, that my husband sleeps in his dressing room, but it's because I sent him there, Eila.'

'But why?' Eila asked the question on a shocked whisper.

Sabina sighed. She hated confiding in Eila or anyone else about David. She loved him too much to talk about him or discuss him at all, but now it was clear that some kind of explanation was called for immediately in case things happened. There was, however, a need for caution. Shani had to be kept out at this stage or the trouble could blow up out of all proportion. True, the girl was the main cause of the rift between David and herself, but bringing her in now could cause pain for others.

Eila and Leif, for instance. They held a good position here at the villa and Leif was working for a career in engineering. Neither must be put in jeopardy. Sabina knew that Eila had become fond of her—one sensed these things. That being so, the woman would need little persuasion to side with her against Shani, and this must not happen for Eila's sake.

With this in mind Sabina tried to make her explanation feasible.

'I know this will sound feeble to you, but I'm afraid the scar on my face is to blame. I'm terrified in case it puts David off making love to me. Some men can't stand anything like that and I don't know if David feels that way about it. I've never asked him. I'm just hoping that I can have my face done soon, that's all.'

Eila shook her head disapprovingly. 'I am sure you are wrong to take this so seriously. You must do as you feel is right, and it is not my business to interfere. I need hardly tell you that your husband has gone out for a swim in the lake and that Shani has followed him there. He told me that you were asleep and that he would not be long.'

Sabina smiled wanly. 'So you woke me with a drink. Bless you, Eila. I'm sure everything will come right in the end. Don't worry about it.'

She sipped her drink when Eila had gone, wondering whether David had planned the early morning swim with Shani. She was thankful now that their marriage had not been consummated. How terrible it would have been to have sought solace in his arms last night and then to receive a confession from him of a love which he was far from feeling for her.

He would never know how her longing for him had kept her awake for most of the night, nor how her limbs turned to jelly at his approach. Her face grew hot at the thought of how she had actually led him on last evening until the arrival of Shani. In a way she ought to feel grateful to the girl not only for opening her eyes about David's feelings but also for appearing at the right time last evening to prevent her from making a fool of herself. The trouble was she loved him as much as ever, and there was nothing she could do about that.

Sabina washed and dressed lethargically, choosing a pretty sun-dress in green gingham. What joy she had derived from buying her trousseau had turned sour and the enchanting picture facing her in the dressing table mirror failed to lift the shadow in her eyes.

The young man sauntering from the lounge downstairs looked up as she descended into the hall. His smile of admiration lifted her heart a little as he whistled softly. He was good-looking, with brown hair and rugged features.

'Well, well,' he murmured audaciously, 'you can't be so cruel as to tell me that you are married? You don't look married. You have an untouched look about you. Yet I can only assume that you must be Mrs Savelon and that the handsome virile male now swimming in the lake is your husband.'

Sabina smiled. 'I'm Mrs Savelon,' she said. 'Who are you? Are you waiting to see my husband?'

'I'm waiting for my breakfast. I arrived last night with Shani—I sat in the car while she came in search of you. You weren't in when we arrived and the housekeeper didn't exactly make us welcome.'

'That was because Shani is supposed to be staying with an aunt in Helsinki while her parents are away. You don't look much older than Shani yourself,' she added.

'I'm twenty-two in years but much older than Shani in other ways,' he assured her. 'Actually I'm here on a walking tour from the U.K. with some other students. Yesterday Shani caught me at a loose end and persuaded me to bring her to collect some of her things from the villa. She told me that a couple were leasing it for a short period.'

Sabina nodded. 'For our honeymoon.'

His mouth dropped open at this and he looked shattered. 'Your honeymoon? Good lord! Shani didn't say so. Look here, Mrs Savelon, I must apologise for barging in on you like this, but I didn't know. I understood you were recuperating from an accident.'

Sabina coloured as he shot a brief glance at the scar on her cheek.

'That's true, and this is Shani's home.' She smiled and put out her hand. 'My name is Sabina. What's yours?'

He took her hand cordially with more than a hint of relief. 'Bill—Bill Sands. Sure you don't mind? There's nothing serious between Shani and me. She's not my type, too spoiled for one thing. But she's good company.'

'I'm sure she is. Shall we go in to breakfast, Bill?'

Bill was saying, 'Nice house this, nicely situated on the sunny side of the lake . . .' when a movement at the front door caused them to turn.

Shani came running in, breathless as though she was being chased.

Snatching off her bathing cap, she cried, 'Bill, you lazy creature, why didn't you come in with us? The water was heavenly. You too, Sabina. I don't know how you can lie in bed. Do you, David?'

David had entered the villa quietly behind her, clad in

his towelling robe. Before he could answer Bill said dryly, 'Did you take a sauna first or just a swim?'

Shani laughed merrily and thrust an arm through David's. 'No, just a swim,' she replied saucily. 'But you never know, next time it could be a sauna as well.'

Sabina looked from one to the other, from Shani whose eyes were shining with an inner excitement to the dark controlled face of David. Those dark eyes of his saw a great deal. She was uncomfortably aware that he had interpreted Bill's question as impudent where he was concerned, but he let it pass. She thought, it serves him right. He asked for it, going out swimming with Shani.

David was saying lazily, 'You'd better go and dress, Shani. That applies to me too.'

Shani returned when Sabina and Bill were half-way through breakfast. Sabina had expected her to take her time in order to dine with David alone, but the girl was more cunning than she thought. She appeared in a striped cotton sun-dress. Her brown legs were bare and her feet were encased in high-heeled sandals. In her scarlet-tipped hands she carried a small neat package which she presented to Sabina.

'A wedding present for you,' she said.

Sabina accepted it politely with a smile. 'Thank you,' she said. 'Please sit down.'

Shani shied away from the table. 'I'll wait for David,' she replied. She watched Sabina place the parcel on the table. 'Aren't you going to open it?'

Sabina's smile was sugar sweet. 'When David comes— it's for both of us. And now do sit down because your breakfast will spoil, and I'm not putting more work on Eila. This is the day she goes to market, so please sit down.'

'Yes, do,' put in Bill. 'Here you are, next to me. I've some questions I want to ask. Why didn't you tell me that Mr and Mrs Savelon were on their honeymoon?'

Shani took her seat with an ill grace and pouted at him prettily.

'Don't look so cross,' she said. 'I didn't tell you because I knew you would want to go shares with me on the wedding present if I did and I knew you hadn't any money to spare.'

Bill's look was frankly disbelieving, but he said nothing. He made a good breakfast, which was more than Sabina did. Shani did not eat much either, preferring to toy with her food until David came. When he eventually put in an appearance he was dressed in his city-going suit and made do with a cup of coffee.

'Sorry I have to go out,' he said. 'See you at lunch time.'

Ignoring Shani's disappointed face, Sabina said, 'I want to speak to you, David, before you go.'

He had downed his coffee and pushed back an immaculate cuff to consult his watch.

'Make it snappy, darling, because I must dash.'

Sabina tried not to wince at the endearment given for the benefit of their guests and stood up to walk with him from the room.

'If you have so little time,' she said, 'I'll go with you in the car.'

He raised a brow. 'But what about your guests?' he asked, looking down at her with some surprise.

Her look at him was stormy. 'Your guests, not mine,' she corrected him. 'I'll fetch my bag.'

He was sitting in the car when she went downstairs again and she slid in beside him. He started the car off without a word, and she sat clutching her bag in her lap as her fury mounted. During the first few minutes of the journey she sat, almost defensively, as it were, holding him at arm's length. Her fragile face was pale but she was determined—so much so that in her eyes lurked a hint of the quality of truth, giving her that serene poise that made her a fit opponent for David.

At last she said in a voice perfectly controlled, 'Why did you ask Shani to stay here at the villa?'

'It seems she came to pick one or two of her personal things up. They did arrive earlier in the evening and it was our fault that they waited so late. There was nothing else I could do since her room was there and a room was available for her friend,' he said evenly.

'And how long does she plan on staying?'

He shrugged. 'I never asked.' A pause while he put on speed as if he found the conversation distasteful. 'Is that what you wanted to talk to me about?'

'Yes. I do think you might have consulted me first before inviting Shani to stay. I mean, if it was for one night I wouldn't mind, but we don't know, do we?'

He said coldly, 'If you remember, you stalked off to bed last night before anything could be said.'

'And I came down this morning to find a strange young man in the house whom I hadn't even met. We might as well have stayed in a hotel if this is what's going to happen. Before we know anything the aunt will be here looking for Shani.'

'What of it? They aren't interrupting anything that I know of. You can hardly say we're on a honeymoon.'

Sabina swung round on him, her eyes blazing. 'That's no reason to advertise the fact of there being a rift between us. How can you be so cool about it, so collected?' She choked back the tears.' You're so blatant about it too!'

'Blatant? About what?'

'About having Shani here. I know what's going on—I'm no fool!'

David ran the car into a layby at the side of the road, switched off the engine, then turned in his seat to look hard at her.

He looked withdrawn, a stranger, and Sabina's heart smote her at the thought of the rift between them widening.

Very quietly he said, 'What am I being so blatant about?'

Uneasiness, faint and nebulous, made her heart beat a fraction quicker. Her mouth went dry and her cheeks burned. 'You know what I mean.'

He looked at her oddly. 'I wouldn't ask you if I knew.' He spoke in the manner of one being reasonable against his will. 'Come on, out with it!'

'Shani.'

'Shani?' He frowned, echoing the name. 'What about Shani?'

'Everything.'

'You mean you don't like her?' He hesitated slightly. 'I'm sorry,' he said, 'but she took me completely by surprise last night. And the hour was very late.'

'You mean you asked her to stay?'

'What else could I do? Apparently she told her aunt in Helsinki that she was coming home for a few days.'

'Wasn't that rather presumptuous on her part, to barge in here when we have the place on lease?'

David shrugged. 'I don't suppose she'll stay long. Besides, she'll be company for you when I'm not here.'

Sabina said shakily, 'But not company for you?'

He stiffened and said sharply, 'Are you implying that I invited Shani here for my own ends?'

White-faced, she answered, 'You certainly didn't invite her for me.'

His hand came beneath her chin, turning up her face to his. 'You and I are married, remember?' His dark eyes raked her smooth young face and shadowed eyes. 'Shani is only a kid.' His smile was tender and mocking. 'You aren't jealous, by any chance?'

'Jealous?' To Sabina this was the last straw. She positively blazed at him. 'Go on, philander with her—but count me out! Goodbye!'

Her hand was on the handle of the car door when his came on top of it. 'Sabina, I've had enough of this. Where are you going?'

'Out for the day. You can expect me back when you see me.'

He lifted his hand from hers then. His eyes were cold and hard. He said curtly, 'I suggest you take a walk to calm down. I want you back at the villa for dinner this evening. You'd better be there.'

Sabina left the car blindly. David had been too clever by half, evading a straight answer to the question of why he had invited Shani to stay at the villa. She drew in a deep breath. She was too inexperienced to read him aright. She had been too bemused by his lazy approach, a laziness that was only a veneer for the vitality which mesmerised her in his voice, his touch, the sudden intent look masking a reserve of latent power from within.

Since her first meeting with Shani it had seemed to Sabina that her marriage to David had become intolerable and unnecessary, and she would no longer hold herself in subjection to it. But in her inmost heart she knew she could not be the one to make the break. That must come from him.

'Mrs Savelon—Sabina—I am delighted to meet you again so soon. Are you alone and, if so, where is that very charming husband of yours?'

The powerful long gleaming car had drawn up silently beside Sabina and she found herself staring down at Anna Hiltunsen at the wheel. She looked chic in a silk-knit white suit. The blue scarf tucked elegantly at her throat was a splash of colour that brought out the gleam in her hair and eyes. Her subtle perfume played tantalisingly in the morning air, and for a few moments Sabina, taken by surprise, stared down at her delicately made-up face. There was an aura about Anna Hiltunsen, the powerful attraction of an arresting personality, she thought. In a way she was not unlike David because there was a hint of the same strong character in both of them. So she could not bring herself to dislike the woman even if she did suspect her of intervening between her son and Kirsty and thus parting them.

Her smile was warm, her manner cordial. 'Yes, I am alone,' she admitted. 'David has gone to some conference or other.'

Instantly one of Anna's beautifully gloved hands opened the car door and with an expressive gesture, she invited Sabina to get in beside her.

She smiled as Sabina settled herself in her seat. 'I too am at a loose end, so we can enjoy the morning together —unless you have other plans?'

Sabina shook her head, welcoming Anna into her loneliness. It was too painful to be on her own at the moment, too painful to have unhappy thoughts nagging at the back of her mind. Anna's presence would keep her mind occupied with other things.

'Forgive me for saying this,' Anna was saying, 'but you do not look happy this morning. Of course, I am very foolish to remark on this, since you find parting from your husband so painful on your honeymoon. However, we can exchange confidences. We may have much to learn from each other.'

Sabina was silent. For some reason she was still on edge where her feelings were concerned, and Anna's arrival had taken her by surprise. Then she told herself that her companion had only an affectionate interest in herself since she was a patient of her son.

'Yes indeed,' she answered, and forced herself to relax. Anna handled the big car confidently. The luxurious leather upholstery creaked faintly and the scented wind, cool against her flushed face, was both comforting and kind.

Anna put on speed, left the village behind and in no time at all was running in to where a restaurant rested at the side of a lake. With great satisfaction, she pulled up and smiled at Sabina.

'This is one of my favourite places,' she said in her warm throaty voice. 'Max and I come here often. We will sit on the veranda overlooking the lake. This way.'

She followed Anna through the dining room where whitewashed walls were graced with photographs of Finnish actors and celebrities to the veranda of tables and chairs. The staff, preparing for a busy day, gave polite bows as they walked past them. Sabina wondered if Anna's photograph was among those adorning the walls and if that could be the reason she had come here. The next moment she was dismissing the idea as being unworthy, for Anna was drawing off her gloves and giving an order to the waiter.

Brightly, she said, 'Coffee is very expensive, as you will have discovered, but I have ordered it because we shall enjoy it. We use cream or lemon in our tea and cream in coffee, which is how it should be. Later we shall partake of lunch in the Finnish fashion. You must learn as much about our country as possible.' Her smile teased. 'When you are with your David I am sure you do not take notice of much that you eat. I well remember the magic of my own honeymoon, and do you know, I could not remember anything of what we ate for our meals.' She laughed, a husky pleasing laugh which Sabina concluded was one of her attractions. 'Do you think that you will?'

Sabina swallowed on a dry throat and tried to answer lightly on what was proving to be a painful subject. 'I shall remember today,' she replied.

The waiter brought small delicacies on paper napkins to eat with their coffee. Anna talked about the country and Sabina gradually relaxed.

Gaily Anna said, 'There is so much to see, and you will find Helsinki very interesting.'

She was an entertaining and amusing companion, and Sabina was prepared to listen to anything she trotted out, providing David was not mentioned. But Anna concluded by saying teasingly, 'Meanwhile the naughty David has left you yet again for this very demanding work of his.'

Sabina felt her face grow hot. She would have liked to point out that she was not asking for Anna's disapproval of David leaving her alone so much. Her resentment at the remark, however, faded at the warmth of the other woman's disarming smile.

'You and David are just right for each other,' Anna went on. 'I envy you your happiness. I only wish I had my husband with me. But I must not complain; I have Max.'

Sabina nodded. 'You've been lucky that Max hasn't married,' she commented. 'I suppose it worries you sometimes whether or not he'll choose the right girl. I know it would me in your place.'

Anna's eyes darkened. 'I shall always have Max,' she said decisively. 'He is part of me. I adore him. It is wonderful how he has taken the place of his father in looking after me.'

The deep-throated voice sounded theatrical to Sabina, who was no longer at one with her surroundings but with Kirsty in spirit and was once again seeing her unhappiness.

'Even so, Max could fall in love and marry,' Sabina said reasonably. 'For instance, when he's at the London hospitals he must meet many lovely women.'

Anna studied the magnificent rings sparkling on her fingers.

'I do not question my son's right to marry if he wished to do so. He does not. He would never leave me.'

She looked up with a strange unfathomable smile as though to say that the subject was closed. Their eyes met and Sabina, emboldened by the thought of the unhappy Kirsty, went on,

'Would you be upset if he married an English girl? I'm curious, that's all.'

Anna's eyes were cold. 'I have never thought about it. Naturally, I would prefer a girl of his own kind since marriage to her would make it easier for them both to adjust to their new life together.'

'In that case I hope that Max does show an interest in

a Finnish girl. Would you encourage the friendship, Mrs Hiltunsen?'

'Certainly not!' Anna went quite pale. 'Max has no friendship with any girl. He would have told me if he had.'

'Would he? Don't you ever worry when he's in London on one of his many visits to the hospitals there? Mrs Hiltunsen, your son is a clever surgeon, a good-looking, charming man of considerable means. He is the kind of man most women dream of marrying. I know, because I saw some of the reaction to him in hospital there. One of these days your son is going to return home with a wife. She could be of any nationality, beautiful perhaps, or plain and sweet, someone who was fortunate to catch him in a lonely moment, and there will be nothing that you could do about it.'

Anna bit her lip. 'You are saying this to frighten me, Sabina. I thought you were my friend. I do not like this kind of talk. We will say no more about it—my morning is quite spoiled. Max was nearly trapped into marriage once by a local girl, but that is now ended, and I will not listen to any more nonsense about him getting married.'

Sabina shook her head. 'I speak to you as a friend who knows how essential it is for your son to marry the right girl. How do you know what he does while he's away from you? He is a normal man with all the normal needs and longings in a man which sometimes have to be assuaged. There's another angle too. Look at it this way. His wife and family could be a comfort to you in later years.'

Anna went pale, recovered herself and asked, 'What kind of a person would you say I was, Sabina?'

Sabina made a vague gesture. 'Extremely attractive, a

magnetic personality with the gift to make almost anyone love you. But you're like most mothers, over-
possessive with your son.'

'In other words, you find me jealous and selfish where
he is concerned?'

Sabina's eyes answered for her. 'Aren't you just a little?
Your son has the right to live his own life as you have to
live yours,' she said.

Anna stiffened. Her voice was on ice. 'You are interfering in something which does not concern you. But I
must bear in mind that you are very young and very
romantic. That being so, I will forgive you even though
our conversation has left me confused. You are raising
doubts in my mind about my son staying with me. Why?'

Sabina gazed steadily at Anna noting for the first time
how the sun penetrated her make-up, the faint tracery of
lines around her eyes, the blurring of her jawline. Was it
the fear of a woman growing old clinging to her son that
prompted her actions where he was concerned? Yet the
serene beauty of her face still held a certain nobility of
character.

Anna, she argued, was a woman who having lost a
husband was claiming the attentions of her son. Her
selfishness, perhaps unrealised in herself, was responsible.
Sabina trembled with the feeling that she was fighting for
the happiness of Max and Kirsty. But even if she was
wrong about them Anna had no right to take over her
son's future.

Sabina said evenly, 'I'm warning you in a way not to
place your future on your son remaining a bachelor.
You're only building up trouble for yourself. He must
have had a desire to marry, otherwise he wouldn't
have become engaged.'

Anna said impatiently, 'Frankly, I could never understand what he saw in the girl.'

'No one ever knows exactly what two people see in each other. Next time he could present you with a daughter-in-law and there would be nothing that you could do about it.'

Anna smiled confidently. 'Max is too fond of me to wish to hurt me, especially with my heart condition,' she replied with some satisfaction. 'You are far too romantic, my child. But I will forgive you because you are in love and wish to see others in love also. You say that no one knows what two people see in each other. I would say that I can see exactly what your husband saw in you. You are not only very young in outlook but you have all the other delightful qualities which a man looks for in a woman. Max sees so many beautiful women in the course of his work that they leave him unmoved. I am sure you are wrong about him.'

Sabina felt saddened in an incomprehensible way. 'Time will tell,' she shrugged. 'And I promise not to say I told you so if I prove to be right.'

Anna laughed. No one would marry her son if she could help it, Sabina thought. But what she had said would take root, she was sure. For the rest of the morning they motored through the beautiful countryside. Sabina blinked at the brilliant lakes through misty eyes, a bright burnished blue shimmering radiance where the sun struck them to their very depths in exotic colours.

They had lunch in a restaurant with the distinctive Finnish flavour of log walls, wooden tables and country rye loaves with a hole in the centre suspended from the ceiling.

'I have brought you here,' Anna told her, 'because

they specialise in regional dishes. I also want you to sample one of our very own liqueurs. Mesimarha, or Mocca as we call it, is made from the berry called *Rubus articus* which is grown in the north of our country. It has a distinctive flavour because it is ripened by the midnight sun and since there are only limited supplies of the fruit we keep it mostly for our own enjoyment.'

A smiling waiter brought the liqueur, presenting it as though he was pleased to give them the means of enjoying themselves. Sipping it under Anna's watchful eye, Sabina felt that the golden glow of the midnight sun was sliding down her throat smooth as cream.

'It's delicious,' she said. In fact the whole meal was delicious, the fresh fish, the hot reindeer tongue served with mushrooms in wickerwork containers of plaited potato straws. The cheeses were different in their presentation and very enjoyable.

CHAPTER SIX

THE long gleaming car had deposited her at the door of the villa and Sabina made her way into the silence of indoors. The moment she opened the door of the room she was conscious of its being occupied. David stood by the window in evening dress, patiently waiting, it seemed, for her return. Tall, broad-shouldered, lean of hip, his face, neck and hands already tanned to a golden brown, he was as fine-looking a man as anyone would wish to see.

'Where have you been?' he asked impatiently. 'Wasn't that Max's car leaving just now?'

'It was.'

'And where have you been with him? Not to the hospital?'

'No. Not with Max. I was with Mrs Hiltunsen. Who were you with?' Sabina threw her bag down on to a chair and walked towards her wardrobe for a wrap.

Roughly he answered, 'You know who I've been with. Need you have left it so late? Our guests are waiting for us.'

She spun round as his voice sounded close behind her. All kinds of vibrations were going on inside her at his unexpected appearance. She was annoyed at his cool assumption that she had kept him waiting, and much more annoyed at the thought of Shani playing a game with her.

She said angrily, 'They're your guests, so why aren't you entertaining them?' Her lips curled contemptuously.

'And don't insult me by pretending that you need my company. I will not be a party to your affair with Shani!'

Her anger sparked off something similar in him, only he was cool, hard and glittering down at her with a set dark face.

'What on earth are you raving about?' he demanded. 'This happens to be Shani's home and it's only natural for her to drop in to pick up a few personal belongings. If you choose to think there's something deeper in our friendship than I care to admit then that's just too bad. The last thing I would have credited you with would be a suspicious mind. But there you are.'

'You're a fine one to talk!' she cried furiously. 'You were ready to believe I'd spent the day with Max. Well, at least I haven't invited him to stay here!'

'And just what do you mean by that?' He gripped her wrists. 'I could shake you! What is it? Have you discovered you prefer Max to me? Is that it?'

'Have you discovered the same about Shani? Let go of my wrists—you're hurting me!'

He said brutally, 'I'd like to hurt you as much as I've been hurt, shake you until those pretty teeth rattle in that empty head of yours. Get changed before I give you a hand towards it. You make me sick!'

He thrust her from him and Sabina massaged her bruised wrists with trembling fingers. Tears forced themselves beneath her eyelids and she turned her head quickly lest he should see them. Then he was behind her, holding her shoulders gently in his hands.

'I'm sorry, darling,' he whispered against her hair. 'You're having a rotten time, what with me being away from you so much and your operation ahead of you.'

Sabina suppressed a shiver. His caress was setting all

kinds of fires alight inside her. It would be so easy to collapse in his arms and pour out her love for him—in other words make a fool of herself. It was so natural to be held back against his heart that she wished time would stand still for ever. His lips were moving from her hair to the side of her neck. Soon they would touch her scarred cheek, and she could not bear that. Muttering something about getting changed, she wriggled from his grasp and fled.

In the bathroom she took a shower and by the time she came out David had gone. All three turned to look at her when she entered the lounge. Shani looked very attractive in pale green, a dress which scintillated but which Sabina thought was too old for her. Her face was made up so perfectly that she must have spent some time on it. But the whole effect was spoiled by the droop of her mouth. It drooped still more as she saw Bill's look of appraisal at Sabina.

Sulkily she took in the chic simplicity of Sabina's dress in white silk jersey, the gold of her hair and the graceful carriage of her slender figure. She gave the smallest of smiles.

'Hello, Sabina. I hope you enjoyed your day out. I suppose one could say that you are taking a working honeymoon, with David being away so much.' Her smile now was full of meaning.

David, however, was completely in command of the situation. He poured out a drink for Sabina, having already given one to Shani and Bill, and moved lightly across the room to give it to her as she sat down. She took it from him, her mind a welter of conflicting emotions.

'You have quite a nice tan,' he remarked. 'It goes well with your golden hair.'

'Yes, doesn't it?' Bill raised his glass. 'Here's to you, Mrs Savelon, all gold and white.'

'Thank you. For a girl with a scarred face that isn't bad,' Sabina smiled, and looked at her husband who had picked up his glass and was standing in a nonchalant attitude with his back against the drinks cabinet. 'Wouldn't you agree, darling?'

She used the endearment deliberately as she saw David's watchful look. He lifted an eyebrow, and it was evident in that moment that he did not care for Bill. Was it because he was jealous of him being with Shani? It could hardly be because Bill was paying her a compliment.

'You make too much of the scar,' he said dryly.

Childishly Shani cried, 'What's the matter with me? Do I have to have a scar before anyone notices little me?'

'Can't bear to be left out, can you, my pet?' Bill taunted. 'Don't you know gentlemen prefer blondes?'

Shani looked shattered and Sabina laughed. 'He's only teasing you,' she said.

Shani appeared to be lacking in a sense of humour. Her look at David was appealing. 'You don't agree with that, do you, David? I thought men liked all kinds of girls. No offence meant, Sabina.'

With practised art Shani addressed Sabina while giving her attention to David. He flicked a glance over his wife and grinned.

'I chose a blonde,' he replied, tongue in cheek. 'Make of it what you will. I'm sure Sabina does.'

If Shani had been a cat she would have had no hesitation in scratching both of them. David's perusal of his wife, taking in the slender figure and golden hair, irked her further. From their first meeting David had been her knight in shining armour. His fine physique, his conservative taste in dress, his attractive goods looks with his six feet plus had set her girlish heart fluttering. He was vital, unforgettable, and he made her come alive.

Her mouth became a line of lipstick. 'Like Bill, you are being perfectly beastly to me, David,' she cried. 'Sabina is my only friend.'

But Sabina was not taken in. It was obvious to her that David was playing up to Shani in order to prove that there was nothing between them. She was as upset as Shani, though for different reasons, and found herself wishing fervently for the evening to end. Desperately she decided to ask Max to bring the date of her operation forward and so bring to an end an untenable situation.

The meal which followed did little to ease the situation for Sabina, with Shani doing most of the talking. Bill too was rather quiet during the evening. What he had seen when Shani was with David had been very disquieting. No young man enjoyed seeing another man evoke a response in his own girl-friend as David Savelon seemed to do. He had never seen Shani come so alive. In any case, it was time he was getting back to his friends in Helsinki.

He broached the subject over coffee. 'I'll be going back tomorrow morning, Shani,' he said. 'My friends will be wondering what's happened to me.'

Shani shrugged. 'Please yourself,' she answered, taking sips of coffee in between smoking a cigarette. 'I haven't seen much of you since we came. You've been tinkering with your car practically all day.'

'Something wrong with it, Bill?'

David's dark brows lifted and Bill looked sheepish. 'Yes,' he admitted. 'If you remember I was tinkering with it on the night I arrived with Shani, which was the reason you thought she'd come alone. I've been trying to repair it myself. Garage repairs cost the earth today and funds just won't run to it, I'm afraid.'

David put down his cup. 'I'll take a look at it if you like. I might be able to help.'

Shani's look of dismay as he rose to his feet was comical. 'Now?' she cried. 'Can't you leave it until morning?'

David said quietly, 'There's no point, is there, if Bill wants to go back to Helsinki early in the morning?'

Shani still had her mouth slightly open after the two men had left the room. 'Good riddance,' she muttered, closing her mouth with a snap. 'Bill's a pain in the neck. I don't know why I brought him in the first place.'

'I was under the impression that he brought you,' Sabina said amiably. 'Why exactly did you come, Shani? You knew your parents would be against it. After all, we are leasing the villa.'

Shani looked waspish. 'I came to pick up a few of my personal belongings, and to see you and David.'

'So you've picked up a few things and seen us. What now?'

Shani moved uneasily, said pettishly, 'You don't seem to realise that I miss my parents. Being here in the villa brings them nearer to me.'

Sabina drank the rest of her coffee. Never for one moment did she believe that Shani was missing her parents. She was much too self-sufficient, too hard, with the selfishness of a thoroughly spoiled child.

'Surely you'll feel as close to them staying with your aunt in Helsinki? Does she know you've come here with Bill?'

Shani stubbed out her cigarette impatiently. Rudely,

she said, 'What's it to do with you?'

'Plenty,' answered Sabina frankly. 'We're responsible for you while you're here.'

'You don't want me here, do you?' The accusation was flung at her malevolently, but Sabina did not flinch. 'You're jealous of David and me. But you will never part us. Can't you see that he is making excuses to be away from you as much as he can?'

'Why don't you be a good little girl and go back to your aunt? I'm sure David will contact you if what you say is true. After all, he can't very well have anything to do with you while you're here. Not in front of me and other witnesses.'

Shani's lips curled contemptuously. 'You mean Eila and Leif? They don't count. They are only servants. I know they don't like me, but I don't care.'

'But then you're not very likeable, are you? Even Bill is beginning to see through you.' Sabina had only been amused at first by Shani's childishness. Now she was thoroughly roused at her sneering reference to Eila and Leif who, in her opinion, were worth two hundred Shanis. Her voice became scathing. 'Incidentally, if you're half as happy in your marriage as Eila and Leif, you can count yourself lucky. They're far nicer people than you will ever be. And all I can say is heaven help any man you might marry. I'll see to it that it's never David.'

Before Shani could recover Sabina was on her way to her room. It was silly to let the girl upset her, she told herself, silly to retire so early too since it was only just after nine o'clock. For a while she paced the room, slowly, unhappily. She was not even allowed a respite from David's presence in the dressing room next door. In order to avoid him when he came upstairs it was necessary for her to be in bed asleep or not.

From her window the sun filled the sky and lake with an aura of gold. Normally she would be out there somewhere with David, strolling by the lake or out in the car to finish off the evening. Instead he was acting as a mechanic to someone's car and she was drifting around like some martyred bride.

For an age she stood watching the sun glittering on the water, the dark green of forests and the villas dotted among them. Everything she had ever heard of about the midnight sun had not prepared her for the breathtaking beauty which now confronted her. The splendid glow engulfed the whole scene which would last through the night, a glorious night leaving no room for sadness. Across the lake people would be dining in the restaurants and perhaps bathing in the enchanting water. Sabina closed her eyes, imagining herself drifting on the lake, and the thought of it spurred her into action.

Changing her dress for a shirt and slacks, she made her way down quickly to the lake. She took the back entrance to the villa and met no one. Sure enough Leif had left the boat out, complete with cushions in case they might go on the lake. She pushed the boat down to the water, stepped in and used an oar to set it sailing. The water was as still as a millpond with the light imperceptibly changing from the hot glare of the day to a more luminous aura that bathed the lake and trees into mysterious beauty.

A night for lovers. Her heart twisted on the thought and she pulled strongly on the oars in a light bright as day but muted. There were people bathing on the far side of the lake; she could hear them as she slid across the water. The breeze ruffled her hair as she rowed, a silent figure of suppressed desperation in the midst of tranquillity. As she rowed Sabina thought about the open-air restaurant on the other side of the lake. It would probably be busy and in order to keep away from the crowds she decided to moor the boat where she would not be seen from there.

As she neared the shore at the far side bathers were frolicking about in the water and several boats were drifting idly about on the surface. Sabina secured the boat in the shelter of overhanging trees and strolled along the shore with a white woolly jacket slung across her slim shoulders. The path was one leading from the crowds, the bathers and the open-air restaurant. Here the pines grew thick not far from the edge of the water and the ground was scattered with fallen cones.

Sabina kicked the cones, staring down at them un-seeingly. Her restlessness was a state of mind that would not go. She was torn between wanting the operation on her face, her love for David, and the work to which he was committed. The rustle of footsteps in the pine needles alerted her to a young couple approaching, and she felt a pang of jealousy at the sight of them with their arms entwined. It was a moment of truth that convinced her about her future happiness. There was none without David. He was her whole life.

She came upon the tall approaching figure unex-pectedly. Like herself, he was strolling along lost in his own thoughts and staring down at the carpet of natural beauty on the ground.

He was hatless and his blond head caught the sun filtering between the trees. Sabina felt her heart lift and she went forward to greet him with a light step and out-stretched hands.

'Max!' she cried. 'What a nice surprise. Are you alone? Your mother is not with you?'

He bowed over her hands as he took them in his. 'This

is indeed a pleasure,' he exclaimed. 'I see you are finding your way around and finding the lake no difficulty. I presume David is somewhere about?'

'As a matter of fact I'm on my own. David is looking at the car of a guest at the villa, so I came for a row on the lake.'

He raised a brow. 'Are you not tired after a day out with my mother? She is out at the moment visiting a friend for the evening.'

Sabina let her fingers curl around the comforting pressure of his.

'No, I'm not tired,' she confessed. 'I enjoyed your mother's companionship very much. Meeting her was quite unexpected and all the more enjoyable for it.'

He nodded. 'The unexpected can be very stimulating for getting the adrenalin working.' His eyes scanned her face, looking young and carefree in the strange sunlit night. Her golden hair had fallen back to reveal the scar on the smooth skin. 'I would like you to keep out of the sun, Sabina, and use the cream I have given you regularly. You are doing that?'

She nodded eagerly. 'Oh, yes. Do I have to wait very long for you to operate? I was going to ask you if you could do it soon.'

He released her hands and lifted her chin to study the scar closely.

Slowly, he said, 'There is no reason why we should wait, but at the moment I have a full list of engagements. Besides, it will mean breaking in on your honeymoon, and I am sure that neither you nor David would want that.'

His smile was most charming, but it did not reach his eyes. It occurred to Sabina in that moment that Max was not a happy man. Like herself he had his problems. She strove to hide her disappointment and at the same time keep up the pretence of a happy marriage.

She said, 'Well, David is out most days. I'm sure he wouldn't mind. I—I would appreciate it if you could fit me in one of these days. Possibly at the hospital in Helsinki.'

'We shall see. And now do come with me to the restaurant for a coffee or a glass of wine. The night is young, and we Finns are reluctant to lose a moment of these long wonderful summer days.'

The thought of going among a crowd of people made Sabina squirm. Her unexpected encounter with Max had jolted her, although she had wanted to meet him so badly in order to discuss an early operation. While she was aware of his calm, stabilising presence, a nebulous depression settled upon her. She was no wiser now than she had been about the date of her operation. The trouble was that if she got into an emotional state about it, like begging him to do the operation as soon as possible, Max would most certainly be convinced that her recovery from the accident was not complete. It was in this state of mind that she allowed herself to be drawn towards the restaurant and the sounds of merriment. Music was coming from the room inside denoting that dancing was in progress. Most of the tables outside were filled with tanned, happy people enjoying themselves, and they hesitated on the fringe of chairs and tables.

'Would you care to dance, Sabina?' Max asked politely.

She looked down at her slacks. 'I'm not really dressed fot it,' she replied, then felt a stab of compunction. As he said, the long summer days had to be made the most of and he had probably been finding the evening as lonely as she had. And he had no suspicion of the cause of her unhappiness, which made it worse.

'If you don't mind my slacks, I'd love to dance.'

With a smile Sabina went into his arms, likening their steely strength to David's. Like David he also conveyed total masculinity and danced with the ease of active muscles. The three members of the dance band played well and Sabina lost herself in the pleasure of the dance. The floor was not too crowded and it was easy to move around. There were no familiar faces around her, so the shock of seeing Kirsty suddenly between the dancers as she appeared near to the entrance almost threw her out of step.

There had been no time for either of them to acknowledge the other. Kirsty had looked a little bewildered, a little afraid at being seen. When the dance number ended, Sabina saw that they were near the open door, but there was no sign of Kirsty. They danced again then Max guided her outside to a table for two.

Their table was on the end of the veranda and Max ordered *marimarja*, the liqueur Sabina had tasted for the first time that day with his mother. He smiled as he handed her a glass.

'Fortunately there are no traffic cops on the lake so you can't be caught for drinking and driving. Only one glass, though. I take it that you are aware of our very strict laws on drunken driving. I am all for it—anyone who is familiar with hospitals usually is. The disfigured cases I've dealt with in my time don't bear thinking about, and many of them were brought about through drunken driving.'

He went on to tell her several of the less gory experiences he had gone through and the time went on wings.

Going back across the lake in the boat, Sabina kept thinking of Kirsty. She had not seen her again in spite of looking around for her, even to going down to the lake again for her return journey. Max had walked with her, helped her into the boat and pushed her off on to the water. Then he had stood watching her row away from him until his tall figure had dwindled in the distance.

The silence of the water was all around her once more, the voices echoing now in the distance with the music from the restaurant. The water dancing with sunbeams seemed to be drawing her into its charmed circle of reminiscences, every one happy. Several birds skimmed across the surface of the water and Sabina drew in deep breaths of pine-scented air. As she neared the villa the smoke curling from the kitchen chimney seemed to wave a friendly greeting. Only the thought of Shani spoiled it.

Drawing nearer to the shore, Sabina grew more and more miserable at the thought of meeting David. She loved him so much that her heart ached for him and what she had done to him by marrying him. He had married her in spite of the fact that he loved someone else. To her, Shani was young and silly, an adolescent blundering her way through calf love. But David obviously saw in her the person he loved. Why else had he not denied any relationship with her?

Then as though her thoughts had reached him by telepathy, he was there to haul in the boat as it touched the shore.

'Where in hell have you been?' he snapped, pulling the boat up on the beach and helping her out. 'I've been searching for you for hours!'

His quiet well-modulated voice had a cold cutting edge to it and she stared at him blankly. He was wearing his working gear, a safari suit of strong twill. In the luminous glow of the sun his features had a satanic gleam, his dark eyes glowed hard as coal, his hair was rough as though he had been raking his hands through it and there was a streak of car oil across his forehead. It was obvious that he had not changed since working on Bill's car.

'But surely you saw that the boat had gone?' she reasoned.

He gestured impatiently with a brown hand. 'Only after I'd searched everywhere for you. If I missed seeing the boat wasn't there it was only because I naturally assumed that Leif had put it away. Why on earth didn't you pass on a message to Shani or Eila?'

'I'm sorry, but I didn't expect to be away so long. Are the others looking for me?'

'Hell, no. What kind of a fool would I have looked if I'd told them that you were missing and I had no idea where you might be? They would naturally assume that something was wrong between us. You go out for the evening and tell no one, not even your husband!'

'It wasn't for the evening.'

'No?' He lifted a dark brow. 'You left Shani at around nine o'clock; it's now well after two in the morning. Come on indoors. I need a drink—the last few hours haven't been exactly pleasant.'

Sabina looked up into his dark face and saw a curious whiteness around his nostrils as though he had received a shock. Was it possible that he had been worried about her? Her heart leapt at the thought and she followed him indoors.

'I'm sorry,' she began as she walked into the lounge,

then looked around in surprise to see no one there. 'Where are Shani and Bill?'

'Gone.' David poured himself a drink, took a sip, then leaned back against the drinks cabinet to regard her with narrowed eyes.

'Gone?' she echoed faintly. 'Shani as well?'

'That's right. Once his car was done Bill saw no reason to wait until morning. I finished the job just before twelve o'clock. Shani made up her mind to go with him at the last moment.'

Sabina clutched the back of the nearest chair dazedly. That white look around his nostrils had not been there for her. It was there because Shani had gone, possibly because they had had a row.

Foolishly, she said, 'We haven't opened her wedding present.' Her eyes moved to a small table to gaze at the unopened parcel. 'I told her I'd open it when you were here.'

'Plenty of time for that,' he said carelessly. 'Now suppose you tell me where you've been. Did you and Shani fall out?'

'No. But I drew the line at spending an evening with her. I went upstairs, decided the evening was too good to be missed and went on the lake.'

'For five hours?' His look was frankly disbelieving.

'No. I went for a stroll along the shore when I got to the far side of the water. It was beautiful and everybody was having a grand time.'

Sardonically, he murmured, 'I'm sure it was. Who did you go to meet? Max?'

'I met Max by accident.'

He flicked his fingers mockingly. 'Let me guess. He was out walking too.'

Her face flamed with colour. 'Now you're being perfectly beastly,' she cried. 'If you insist on being insulting I'm going to bed!'

'I shouldn't if I were you,' he warned with a dangerous glint in his eyes. 'We should only carry on this conversation upstairs and you might not like the outcome in such intimate surroundings.'

She trembled. He was looking at her with an expression she could not interpret—searching, quizzical, bitter? It could be a mixture of all three. Retreating imperceptibly, she said with assumed coldness, 'Max was out walking. His mother was out. He asked me to go for a coffee at the outdoor restaurant, and we joined in the dancing there.'

His eyes glittered as he finished the rest of his drink. 'For someone who's anxious to avoid crowds you surprise me. Go on.'

He put down the empty glass and pushed his hands into his pockets. His dark gaze was on her, making her feel defenceless and very young.

She said, 'I wanted to see Max to ask him about the operation on my face.'

'What did he say?'

'He's going to let me know when he can do it. He's a bit tied up at the moment with work.'

His dark ironic gaze, still with that expression she could not read, filled her with discomfort. The silence stretched out as he meant it to do and she tilted her chin.

Slowly, he said, 'I see. You aren't falling for Max by any chance, are you? I don't have to be very intelligent to realise that being your doctor puts him in a rather special light where you're concerned. He's sympathetic, he puts you at your ease and he's going to erase the scar.'

'Very, very funny,' she snapped.

'It all happens to be true.' He straightened indolently away from the cabinet to his graceful height. 'And that isn't an answer.'

Sabina gave him a defiant stare. He was standing there irresolute, waiting . . . and her heart jumped.

Defensively, she said, 'Max is a friend.'

She wanted to ask him what he was—lover, cynic, friend, husband or the stranger he appeared to be right now who was eyeing her with a hard accusing look. She couldn't, of course, for in spite of his antagonism, the tousled dark hair, his oil-streaked face gave him an oddly boyish look which tore at her heart. A sudden wave of tenderness washed over her, as sharp and exquisite as a pain. I love him so much, she thought despairingly with a rush of passionate feeling. Why don't I tell him so? But he was miles away from her. There was no touching him.

With a cynical twist of his lips, he said, 'I'll go for a wash.'

Sabina stood still for a long time after he had gone upstairs trying to sort out her distorted thoughts. Head and heart ached, but she had to go on in the same unsatisfactory circumstances. David was retreating more into himself. She had changed too. She was not the happy girl who had flung herself into his arms at each joyful meeting. The sun, muted now, with fingers of light stiffly spread across the room, sent a shiver across her body. Shani's wedding present, unopened, was before her on the small table. She had been dreading opening it. Now she tore it open with trembling fingers.

It was a kitchen wall clock and Shani had written a message with it. 'To David who taught me how precious time is. Love, Shani.'

All was quiet when she entered their room. Then David was there coming from the bathroom. He wore a towel tucked in at his waist. Sabina tried to ignore the rippling muscles beneath a skin which shone like bronze satin.

She was not aware that she was staring until he spoke.

'You don't mind me appearing in just a towel, do you?' he asked with some sarcasm. 'At least we're married, and it makes a change from seeing you in bed on my way in or out. The visions I saw were very alluring. However, I forgot to take my bathrobe into the bathroom with me.'

She broke the electric silence by saying, 'Shani's wedding present, a kitchen clock. There's a note . . . for you.'

She proffered the note, still clutching the present. She held it at arms' length as though to keep her distance from the tall bronzed figure coming towards her with his long graceful stride. David's dark hair fell in damp tendrils on his forehead and he laughed as he read the note.

She quivered and above the frightened beating of her heart she was aware of the whiteness of his teeth against his tan. His eyes challenged hers.

'At least it's something we haven't had—or have we had a kitchen clock?'

Sabina dropped her gaze. 'No, we haven't. I shall have to send her a thank-you note.'

'Yes, do that,' he answered laconically, and strode to his dressing room. At the door he halted and turned to face her. 'I've asked my two colleagues for dinner at eight. You might talk over the menu with Eila.'

CHAPTER SEVEN

SABINA had written a few letters, had sent Shani a thank-you note for the wedding present, and was leaving the kitchen after discussing the dinner to be given that evening for David's colleagues. David had gone out before she was up and she was going out to post her letters when a car drew up outside.

The woman who appeared on the threshold looked to be in her late twenties. She wore a cotton dress in apple green edged with white. A triangular scarf of the same material held back the tawny hair. Her green eyes were warm and friendly and one of the pink-tipped hands was outstretched in greeting while the other held her shoulder bag in place.

'Good morning. I'm Sally May Minton. My husband Skip is a colleague of David's. Is he anywhere around?' Her accent was a hundred per cent American. 'You must be Sabina, David's wife.'

'Yes, I am.' Sabina took the newcomer's hand cordially in hers. 'David has mentioned you. Won't you come in?'

In the lounge Sally May seated herself, crossing long slim legs, and slipping her shoulder bag to the floor. Sabina hovered, smiled, then said, 'Can I offer you a drink? Coffee?'

'No, thanks. You know, you're rather what I expected —young, sweet, and deliciously feminine. Tell me, dear, aren't you finding this project our husbands are confined to a terrible bore? I'm beginning to ask myself whether I have a husband or not!'

Sabina smiled, having found a kindred spirit. 'I am too,' she admitted.

Sally May nodded. 'Poor girl! Not much of a honeymoon for you. Where is David, by the way? I expected to find him at home making the most of his day off from work with you.'

Sabina felt a cold dew gather on her temples. A sickness rose in her stomach. This had to happen, she told herself. She ought to have been prepared for it. Her legs let her down into the nearest chair.

'David is out at the moment. Did you want to see him particularly?' She willed suppleness into a stiff jaw. 'He —he won't be long.'

Sally May glanced briefly and impersonally at Sabina, who was wearing a pastel blue trouser suit that echoed the blue of her lovely wide-spaced eyes. If she had noticed the scar on her cheek she took good care that her expression did not change.

'I'm so sorry, Mrs Savelon,' she began, and looked apologetic, 'but I'm afraid my husband and I can't make it for dinner this evening. My parents are due to arrive today. They're on a world cruise and are coming to spend a few days with us. I could have called you on the telephone, but I felt I had to come personally to make my apologies. We had a cable early this morning.'

'Could you not bring your parents with you this evening?'

Sally May shook her head regretfully. 'Skip and I did think about it, but these world cruises take a lot out of one, and we decided it was important for them to rest while they're with us.'

Sabina nodded. 'I understand.' Her pulse was beating back to normal. 'I'm sorry you can't come—I'm sure we would have enjoyed your company. David will be disappointed.'

Sally May smiled. 'I'm sorry we didn't make your acquaintance earlier, but as you're on your honeymoon we thought you would object to people butting in. Also my days have been full since I arrived. I'm a gregarious type of person, so my engagement book is pretty full. We must get together when my parents have gone. We're very fond of David,' she added. 'He's a clever engineer. Skip admires him greatly and I love him.'

She laughed huskily. Sabina felt drawn towards her. 'Then we have something in common, Mrs Minton, because I love my husband too.'

'Call me Sally May, please, and I'll call you Sabina. It's much more friendly.'

'Lovely. Did you meet David on his previous brief visit here just before we were married?'

Tentatively Sabina met her visitor's frank gaze. This was something she had to know.

'Oh, yes. We've been here for some time. We dined with Mr and Mrs Somers from whom you lease this villa before they left for America. I don't know if you've met their daughter Shani. She's something of a liability. I'm glad David is keeping an eye on her while they're away.'

'Keeping an eye on her?' Sabina froze, echoing the words.

'Yes. When I've picked my husband up after a conference, Shani has been there waiting for David. Frankly, Sabina, I wouldn't have the girl in my house or within miles of my husband.'

Sabina had to stand up then to move as though to call Eila. 'You must have something to drink,' she said. 'Coffee? Do say yes. I feel awful not giving you some kind of refreshment.'

Her visitor consulted her wristwatch. 'Coffee, then, please. I mustn't stay long—I'm picking Skip up. He's having a haircut, so I have to be quick.'

Sabina went quickly to the kitchen to find Eila placing some pastries attractively on a plate, having already made the coffee. She had heard the car arrive and acted accordingly. Sabina told her what had happened, then carried the tray into the lounge herself. The short respite had given her time to digest what her visitor had said. Only now was she beginning to fully appreciate Sally May's visit. It was in the form of a timely warning about Shani. She was grateful, but she had to go warily.

'Just cream. No sugar, thanks.'

Sally May watched as Sabina served the coffee with a remarkably steady hand. She passed her visitor the pastries and sat down to take a drink of coffee herself, after which she felt better.

'How do you like it here?' Sally May nibbled a pastry and looked approvingly around the beautifully furnished room. 'I love this villa.'

'I do, and I love the lake being so near.' Sabina paused, said in quite ordinary tones, 'Here we have the solitude I want. I'm not the gregarious type and neither is David.'

Sally May shrugged. 'It wouldn't do for us all to be alike. After all, you are on your honeymoon. Don't you find the midnight sun a little eerie? And the winters here must be frightful with very little daylight. We went to Florida for our honeymoon. Incidentally, I wish you both much happiness.'

Where her own brightness was drawn from Sabina did not know. She drank her coffee, talked and laughed as if she was the happiest of brides. Fortunately her guest was fond of talking and could make a conversation interesting.

Not that Sabina listened to everything—how could she, when all the time she was wondering about David. Why he had not told her that he had the day free, and where had he gone?

The sound of a car arriving and the door slamming still did not prepare her for his arrival. He strode in looking bright-eyed, healthy and extremely attractive. He was wearing a continental shirt and light, summer-weight belted slacks. A silk scarf was knotted in careless elegance at his firm brown throat. His eyebrows shot up when he saw his visitor.

'This is something like a welcome,' he said. 'Two pretty girls. Any more coffee left?'

'Yes. I'll go for another cup for you.' Sabina made as if to rise, having put down her empty cup, but David forestalled her.

'I'll use yours,' he said, and she poured it for him.

His smile included them both. 'You and Skip are coming to dinner this evening, I take it?'

Sally May finished her coffee and put down the empty cup. 'Sorry, David—that's why I'm here. My parents are coming today for a rest from their world cruise. It's a long time since I saw them.' She looked at her watch in dismay. 'Goodness, I have to fly! Skip will be waiting for me.'

They both went to see their visitor off, David with an arm draped carelessly around Sabina's shoulders. It was on her mind to ask him about Shani meeting him after his conferences, until she realised that he would only tell her what he wanted her to know.

'Any plans for today?' he asked.

They were on their way indoors and his arm had dropped from her shoulders, leaving them strangely cold in the warm air.

'None,' she answered. 'Apart from going out to post some letters and Shani's thank-you note for her present.'

'They aren't urgent, are they?'

'No.'

'Good. Then what about taking a picnic on the lake? There's a small island that looks ideal not far from the shore. I'll see Eila about a picnic basket while you go for your beach bag.'

When they went down to the shore Leif was coming back from putting cushions in the boat which stood at the ready.

'Have a nice day,' he said with a shy smile.

They exchanged a few pleasantries and went on their way.

'He's nice, isn't he?' Sabina said.

David glanced down at her mockingly. 'Is he your kind of man?' he asked with satire. 'Shy, reserved and tractable. He wouldn't give you any trouble such as making demands which you couldn't meet.'

Sabina bit her lip. They were on dangerous ground and this was only the beginning of their day together. Whatever happened he must not be allowed to bait her. She must keep her cool.

There was a devil in David that could spring to life when challenged, she knew. Not that he was unreasonable; he could be the most gentle, teasing person. He was generous almost to a fault and his sense of humour made him very endearing. Unlike Leif he was arrogant and rocklike in his manner and he had admitted to being an insatiable man. Yet he was too self-disciplined, too well-balanced to be other than a gentleman. And therein lay his potent attraction to women, including herself.

She said, 'Why didn't you tell me you had the day free?'

'I wanted to surprise you. That's why I rushed off to the post office this morning to send off important letters.'

Indignantly she cried, 'You could have posted mine.'

'Not a chance. I had to catch the early post.' He dropped the paraphernalia for a picnic into the boat, then helped her in. 'You were saying about Leif.'

'I wasn't—you were,' she contradicted.

David took the oars and pushed off from the shore, and to her surprise Sabina found herself smiling. So he had not gone to see Shani after all.

'Is that tender smile for Leif or for me?'

His deep voice broke into her thoughts and she answered him at random.

'You appear to have gone slightly sour on Leif—I don't know why. He could be more dynamic than he looks. In any case, no woman has a special kind of man in mind when she falls in love. It just happens, and any images she has hitherto formed in her mind are forgotten in the magic of an encounter with the one man in her life.'

A trifle acidly, he said, 'You're talking about physical attraction. Beware—it's a two-faced trap.'

'Not when the chemical reaction is the same on both sides.'

His glance at her was calculating. 'You mean the kind of stuff that explodes,' he said with heavy sarcasm. 'Ours appears to have gone off like a damp squib.'

Sabina shrank inwardly from the bitterness of his voice. In spite of her resolution not to rise to his baiting, she had done just that.

The lake was not so deserted today. At the far side outside the open-air restaurant people were bathing, boats were out in force and there were several water-skiers. But David was rowing to a small island of greenery to the left edged by a sandy shore.

The island was not deserted, for there were boats moored in various sheltered spots. Sabina relaxed, but it was a gradual process. A cautious joy rippled through her veins. This was heavenly, to be alone with David away from the villa. Here they were bound by the sweet bond of natural beauty, the luminous water smooth as cream, the pines giving off their aromatic scent as they stood like sentinels reflecting their image in the lake, the birds skimming across the surface to disappear among green, mysterious foliage.

Not that Sabina had anything against the villa. It was just that Shani's image was there; there was no getting away from it. She closed her eyes, feeling her hair lifting gently in silken fronds in the breeze. Seeing people already occupying the island had not worried her, which posed a question, or was it two? The first was: could she be learning to live with the scar? The second: had David deliberately brought her here in order that they would not be entirely alone? The presence of other people made it fairly certain that there would be no repetition of the other incident when they had gone rowing and she had run away from his embrace. He pulled in at a small stretch of beach where trees gave shade and large white rocks provided shelter from any wind.

It was David who carried everything to the shade of trees and it was he who suggested a swim before lunch. He had evidently put his bathing trunks on beneath his slacks, which he peeled off and was soon in the water.

Sabina was more casual, unbuttoning her cotton dress and kicking off her sandals. David had disappeared when she slid into the water, presumably to swim around the small island. She swam out, making for the other side of the lake, piqued because he had not waited around for her. Then, anxious not to spoil their day, she turned on an afterthought and followed him around the island. As she turned a hot pain shot through her right knee. She had wrenched it. At first the pain was so acute that she went under, then gradually it eased a little, but swimming was agony.

There was nothing for it but to make for the beach of the island. Fighting down a panic hurting her throat, Sabina pushed the water out of her way and struck out for the shore. At last she was gasping her way to a small deserted stretch of beach around the corner from where their boat was moored. Then she was lying on the sand, her whole body shuddering with painful gasps.

It was some time before Sabina sat up to examine the injured knee. There was no sign of injury, for it looked normal enough, and she began to massage it very gently. After a while she flexed her leg and found there was no further pain. While it was a great relief the thought came that it would be better to walk back across the island instead of swimming around to the other side. There was no assurance that the knee could go again. Besides, a walk was the therapy necessary to sort out her jumbled thoughts.

Treading carefully with her bare feet on the moist damp ground, Sabina felt suddenly carefree and happy. Here in lovely surroundings with the birds and their songs for company there was no room for gloom. Now and then she stopped to pick the small pink and white flowers which grew between the white rocks.

Her sense of direction brought her eventually to where they had moored the boat. The picnic basket was still at the foot of the tree where David had placed it but he was nowhere about. Putting down the flowers on the grass, Sabina spread out the cloth, put out paper napkins and cutlery. Then David came striding on shore from the water and pushing his hair back with an impatient hand. Scooping up a towel, he dried himself and gave his hair a rub.

'Enjoy your swim across the lake?' he said grimly. 'I trust Max was waiting for you.'

'I didn't go across the lake,' she answered, putting out cups and plates. 'I followed you around the island.'

'I saw you go.' He flung down the towel and lowered himself on to the ground beside the picnic. 'I seem to remember the time when you were dead against crowds. Not long ago, is it, only since your accident?'

Sabina put out the rest of the things Eila had provided. A pulse was hammering at the base of her throat. 'It seems years ago. Maybe I'm beginning to learn to live with it.'

'Oh, sure. When you're with Max. Why not with me?'

'I'm with you now, and I didn't go across the lake to see Max.'

Sabina was determined not to tell him about injuring her knee and her walk across the island. He was so ready to think the worst of her that she was going to let him go on thinking it. He said no more and they ate their lunch in silence.

Afterwards David lay flat on his back and closed his eyes. Sabina sat for a long time looking across the lake. Then she lay down, careful to keep the picnic things between them. She was awakened by water-skiers skimming across the water and sat up to watch them swerve around and make for the opposite shore.

David stirred and said, 'What about a paddle around

the island? Too soon for a swim after lunch.'

He turned his head to squint at her in the bright sunlight. His dark hair had dried in crisp buoyancy. He looked big, brown and uncaring in his swimming trunks. Like her, he was unsettled when once he had been content with her company. Once they had not been able to look at each other without smiling. They had always been on the edge of laughter because most of their likes and dislikes coincided. They both hated cockroaches, liked spiders, and going for long walks. Now all that had gone, bewilderingly and for ever. A sweet relationship had gone sour before its fulfilment, and all because David had made that fateful visit here a week before their marriage. The tragedy of it was that she loved him far too much to want to end the present untenable situation.

'If you like,' she answered without much expression. After gathering up the remnants of their lunch and putting all their paraphernalia under the tree, David reached for her hand and they waded into the cool water. Paddling through the water with David was something she had not envisaged. His hand was warm and strong and his fingers curled around hers as they swished through the water. Although the sun was warm Sabina felt cold inside. She was close to him and yet not close at all.

She had forgotten her injured knee and was quite unprepared when it suddenly let her down. Stifling a cry of pain, she clung to him in an effort to keep on her feet.

'Steady on!' he exclaimed, suddenly supporting her. 'What is it? Have you hurt your foot?'

'My knee,' she gasped. 'It gave way. I shall be all right in a moment. I think I twisted it.'

Scooping her up in his arms, David strode back with

her to the shade of the tree, then lowering her down gently he sat down beside her and examined her knee.

The feel of his warm flesh against her had filled her with anguished longing for the ardent warmth of his lips. The pain in her knee in those few precious moments when she was held close to his heart had almost been an ecstasy.

His fingers were warm and gentle. 'Tell me where it hurts,' he said, exploring round her kneecap with a very slight pressure. The gentle massage eased the pain and he said softly. 'Now suppose you tell me where you twisted it. You didn't do it just now, did you? It seemed to me that the knee deliberately let you down.' His comprehensive glance was wary as if he was trying to obliterate her girlish figure in the two-piece swimsuit. 'Has it happened before?'

Sabina lowered her eyes to the lean brown fingers on her knee. 'I twisted it badly when I was swimming just now. I was piqued because you'd gone off without me and had decided to swim across the lake—it isn't far from the island here. Then I thought better of it, turned round to follow you around the island and hurt my knee.'

'Go on.'

'I managed to get back to the shore, then I walked across the island back again. I picked the flowers on the way.'

She looked towards the small bunch of pink and white flowers on the grass not far away. But David did not turn his head. His mouth pulled in with anger.

'Why on earth didn't you tell me? And why did you agree to come now on this walk through the water? You might have known that the knee was likely to go again. It needs rest. There's no actual damage from what

I can see, but you never know, since I'm no doctor. I'm going to take you back to the villa and call one.'

'But I don't want a doctor,' she protested. 'The knee will be fine if I rest it.'

David stood up as if she had not spoken. 'I'll go and dress,' he said.

When he came back Sabina had put on her button-through dress and he picked her up to carry her to the boat. After settling her down comfortably among the cushions he went back for the lunch things and pushed out the boat.

Sabina was not worried about her knee. She was one of those lucky people who seldom had anything wrong with them. David was just being masterful. Considering the agony of mind she had suffered over her scarred face, she reflected, the injury to her knee was a very minor one.

David asked her several times during the short journey back to the villa if her knee was hurting, and she shook her head. It seemed to her that his manner towards her had changed. He looked more like he had on their first meeting, his eyes gently mocking, his well-cut mouth on the verge of a teasing remark. She badly wanted to smile back at him, to yield to the dictates of her heart, but he had married her while loving someone else, and she could not forget that.

She said, 'About dinner this evening, who's coming? Urfo and Kirsty?'

He shrugged. 'I can put them off if you like, since Skip and Sally May aren't coming.'

Reasonably, she said, 'Why should we put them off? Why not ask Max and his mother in their place, that is if they're available.'

'Meaning that you prefer Max to look at your knee?'

'Why not? He's a medical man—he took up plastic surgery after he'd qualified.' She quivered at the sardonic expression on his dark face and wondered whether he was using Max to widen the rift between them. 'I don't want a doctor to look at my knee—it's you who's insisting.'

The silence seemed interminable. Sabina tried to appear detached, and felt David studying her. But he said no more. When they got back to the villa he scooped her up into strong arms and carried her into the lounge. Then he went to the telephone. Max was not at home, neither was his mother, the housekeeper informed him.

David strode into the lounge looking across to where Sabina sat in the roomy chair looking small and vulnerable with the sunlight streaming across the room on to her golden hair.

'There's no one at home, but I've left a message. I could call another doctor,' he said tersely. 'That knee wants seeing to.'

She said hurriedly, 'It's not that important, and it is my knee. If I can't see Max then I'll see no one. And it's not bad at all. I've simply twisted it or sprained it. I have no pain now and I can walk on it.'

She got to her feet to prove her point and stood up quite normally.

David looked at her, not entirely convinced, then said grudgingly,

'All right, you've proved your point. One thing is for sure, though, you aren't to go swimming unless I'm with you. Is that understood?'

Sabina nodded and lowered her head; she found his regard too disturbing. He had to play the role of a fond husband, of course, but she wished he would act more in character as a man in love with another woman.

'I'm going to see Eila about dinner this evening,' she said. 'I think we'd better cater for six after all in case Max and his mother come.'

He shrugged as though he did not care one way or the other. 'I'm going out. Suit yourself. I won't be long.'

But he was. Sabina had washed and changed for the evening when he returned. He stopped short as he walked into their room to flick a glance over her slim figure, enchanting in the simple cap-sleeved white cotton lace dress with scallop-edged trim to the full skirt. Her hair was silky and shining around a delicate face which now had the sudden bloom of a tea-rose beneath his scrutiny.

'How's the knee?' he asked brusquely. 'Sorry I'm late.'

'It's all right,' she answered, turning to pick up the matching lace stole to her dress from where it lay on the bed.

Strange, she thought, but no matter how she drilled herself for his appearance, the effect was always electric. His dark eyes, with that deep intense look, never failed to make her spine tingle, her pulses race. And all this for a man who had probably just slipped out to see another girl, Shani.

As he noticed her action his eyes narrowed. 'You'd better wait for me to accompany you downstairs in case your knee gives out.'

He had not finished speaking before a car was heard to arrive and she went to the window. Urfo and Kirsty were getting out of their car, and without turning, Sabina said, 'I'm going down. Our guests have arrived.'

'Go by all means,' he answered curtly. 'You mustn't keep Max waiting, must you?'

As the door of his dressing room closed behind him Sabina drew her lace stole about her shoulders and went downstairs. They were admitted by Eila and Sabina went forward eagerly to greet them. Kirsty was looking very attractive in tan silk and Urfo was his usual friendly self.

Sabina had felt her knee a little as she went downstairs, but that was all. They exchanged greetings and were about to go into the lounge when a second car drew up outside, and Max came in. Taking in the situation at a glance, he recovered quickly and came forward to greet Sabina warmly.

'What's this about an injured knee?' he asked after the usual greeting. 'Mother is away for a few days and actually I came from the hospital. Do you wish me to look at it now?'

'Goodness, no!' Sabina exclaimed. 'After dinner, please. You are staying to dinner?' Her wide blue eyes scanned his good-looking face with concern. 'We haven't taken you away from something important, I hope?'

He shook his head. 'Not at all. The message came through from my house, so I called on my way there.' He looked down at his summer-weight city-going suit. 'I did not have time to change.'

Sabina said lightly, 'You always look immaculate. There are only five of us, an uneven number, but we're all friends. Come along into the lounge. David will be down soon.' She linked Max by the arm and led the way, avoiding the reproachful look in Kirsty's eyes as she did so.

Max presided over the drinks at Sabina's request and she noticed that Kirsty kept close to her brother when they sat down by taking a seat by him on the sofa. Max could not have timed his entrance at a more awkward

moment, she thought. There had been no time to warn
her that Max might be coming, not even after she had
rushed downstairs on seeing them arrive. Sabina's eyes
rested gently on Kirsty's quiet figure, taking in the dark
shiny hair, the lucid brown eyes, the small, appealing
face with nothing much in the way of outstanding
features, but a whole which spelt charm and a smile that
illuminated.

'Kirsty, Urfo.' Max was bending over them with drinks
on a tray. 'Your drinks. I do not forget what you like.'

Kirsty accepted hers politely with a small smile. Urfo
was courteous but cool. Addressing Sabina, he said, 'I
understood that Skip and his wife were coming.'

Sabina accepted her drink from Max and sat down
beside Kirsty on the sofa. 'They were,' she said. 'Unfortunately they had to cancel it at the last moment.'

As she explained the reason for Skip not coming,
Sabina noticed Kirsty's hand shaking as she held her
drink. Her face was pale and strained. It was obviously
an ordeal for her to meet Max again. They had probably
become adept at avoiding each other at parties or any
social gatherings. Poor Kirsty! She evidently had not
recovered from their unhappy affair. And what about
Max? He did not appear to be concerned over his ex-
fiancée's presence, or was he better at masking his
feelings?

Sabina had nothing to go on but her own womanly
intuition. To her they were two very nice people who
seemed made for each other, and who had been parted
by some unkind hand of fate. Was she right in interfering,
in deliberately insisting on Max coming this evening
because Kirsty would be there? David would not think
so. He was already of the opinion that she had rushed
downstairs to meet Max.

David walked into the room at that moment looking dark and vital in his evening clothes. His keen dark eyes took in his guests at once, his white smile included Sabina.

'Hello, Kirsty, Urfo. Glad you could make it. You too, Max. Where is Mrs Hiltunsen?'

'Away for a few days with friends.' Max dropped ice into two glasses, asked David what he wanted and filled them up. Neither man sat down but stood talking. When they engaged Urfo in their conversation, Sabina spoke hurriedly in undertones to Kirsty.

'Sorry I couldn't warn you about Max coming. We weren't sure if he was.'

Kirsty had rather a strange look, she somehow looked thinner, and minus her usual sparkle. 'Do not worry,' she said with a pale smile. 'It was just one of those things. We live through them, so let us forget all about it. I am sorry you hurt your knee,' she added. 'Does it pain you?'

'No, just lets me down occasionally. David got all fussy and insisted upon me seeing a doctor. I wanted Max seeing that I know the man, but he was out when David telephoned.'

Kirsty said thoughtfully, 'Strange that I have done the same thing. I twisted round suddenly on the ward in the hospital when a patient called me the other day. The pain was killing for a second or so. My left knee is still a little swollen.'

'What did the doctor say when you told him?'

'I have not told a soul except you. It is no matter. The knee will go right again. Like yours, it does not pain me.'

'What are you two whispering about?' David asked, his dark eyes moving from one to the other.

'We're comparing injuries like pulling a muscle in the knee,' Sabina said lightly.

Max raised a light brow. 'You have the same malady?' he questioned politely.

Kirsty's face went crimson. 'It is not important in my case.'

She did not look directly at Max but talked to her drink, looking down into the glass. Her precise English was one of her charms, had she but known it. But Max was not the only one to regard her with some concern.

Her brother Urfo said, 'I noticed you were limping slightly when you arrived from the hospital today.'

Kirsty looked daggers at her brother seated beside her on the sofa.

She said indignantly, 'I was not limping. I am perfectly all right!'

Leif came in at that moment to announce that dinner was ready and they all trooped into the dining annexe where the rectangular table of polished wood gleamed softly with silver and crystal glass. David sat at the top end of the table to make the numbers even, with Sabina by Max on his right and Kirsty with Urfo on his left.

The dinner had to be a success because everything was cooked and served so beautifully. Sabina, glancing around at the guests, decided that the only really happy person present was Urfo, who sat stolidly eating and enjoying each course.

Kirsty, Sabina noticed, seldom lifted her eyes from her plate except to talk to her brother and not once did she look across the table at Max. He, however, looked across at her quite often when she was unaware of his regard.

The meal had got off to a bright start with David talking to Leif of his forthcoming engineering exams at the university. Urfo surfaced from his happy state to question him about it, offering to lend him books on the subject or anything else that would help. Everybody seemed to relax, or rather Sabina felt that they did, with the exception of Kirsty. What a different person she was with her eyes full of laughter. If only she would smile! Then Sabina realised that she did not feel much like smiling herself. Philosophically she told herself that she would feel different when the scar on her face was gone. But with poor Kirsty the scar was on her heart.

After dinner Max suggested taking a look at Sabina's injured knee. David and Urfo had got into a discussion concerning the project they were engaged on and had temporarily left the room to look at some plans which David had completed.

Sabina lifted the skirt of her evening dress while Max carried out a routine inspection of the injured knee. A beam of sunlight coming in through the tall windows caught the side of his powerful blond head as he bent over her. He looked strong, very sure of himself and his knowledge, as if at that moment he did not need, was oblivious to, human contacts.

In a welter of emotion Sabina thought how awful it would be for someone to love him and to know that love was not returned. She was not given to interfering in the emotions or complexities of other people. To her they had never seemed on the surface to be other than straightforward and uncomplicated. But the awareness of the still quiet figure of Kirsty near to her hit her with painful intensity. With Max there, seemingly unaware of her, the situation became more disturbing.

'Hmmm,' said Max, and the spell was broken.

Sabina glanced up at him expectantly as he straightened and turned his blue searching gaze upon her.

'Nothing much wrong. You've pulled a tendon behind the knee. Rest is w! at it requires. Not too much walking or swimming.' He paused, smiled, then added, 'Fortunately you can rest. Unlike Kirsty here you have no exacting job to keep you on your feet most of the day.'

His smile included Kirsty seated beside her on the sofa. 'Am I correct in assuming that you have also injured your knee?' he asked her suavely.

Kirsty looked distressed. 'It . . . was nothing, I assure you.'

Max looked at her in the startling way he had when he was either interested or moved.

'Your brother said you were limping earlier when you arrived at your villa, did he not?'

Reluctantly Kirsty agreed and said hastily. 'There is no reason why you should concern yourself over it. I have a fortnight's vacation from the hospital starting from now, so if my knee troubles me again I can rest it as much as I please.'

'So it has troubled you? How recently?'

Kirsty threw an agonising look for help from Sabina, who suddenly looked wide-eyed, interested and serene.

'Not recent or important enough for me to discuss it with any of the doctors at the hospital,' she said desperately.

'Yet you told Sabina. Was it so much on your mind that it just slipped out?' He smiled. 'Come, Kirsty, stop playing games. A brief examination right now can allay all your fears. Well, what about it?' he finished abruptly. His warmth and charm were gone and he was once more a practised surgeon as he looked full at her.

It was Sabina who broke the electric silence. 'Yes, come on, Kirsty. Show those lovely long legs of yours to Max.

The poor man needs a break from looking at scars and skin grafts.'

For answer Kirsty began, not without trepidation, to follow Sabina's example and draw up her evening skirt to reveal a long and shapely leg. Sabina watched Max cast an impersonal eye at her leg as a matter of course, and thought ruefully that to him it was all in a day's work. She was conscious first of a deep unbroken silence as his fingers moved with a sure touch unfalteringly over Kirsty's knee. Yet she sensed a feeling of tension, a tension caused more by Kirsty's embarrassment than by Max's sudden abruptness.

There had to be something between these two very nice people who had known each other such a long time. Her instinct told her that Max was conscious of it, Kirsty too. It would be easy, only too fatally easy, to interfere and turn what was a delicate situation into a tragedy again by parting them with well-intended help. Sabina had always maintained that do-gooders on the whole wrought more havoc than those less well intentioned.

Glancing at Max, she saw his jaw was purposeful, his glance keen. He straightened. 'There appears to be a little fluid under the kneecap. I am going to prescribe pills to take it away.' He paused, and added, 'It should be gone in a few days providing you take them. Being a nurse, I am sure you will agree that a pill taken in time saves nine.'

Kirsty made no reply. She was looking up into his gaze in a way that made words unnecessary—exciting, dangerous, as though two people who had parted had suddenly found themselves again.

But if Sabina imagined they were going to throw themselves into each other's arms she was mistaken. Max consulted his watch, and said, somewhat regretfully, that he had to leave. Kirsty and Urfo did not stay long after Max had gone.

David said cynically, 'I think they're conscious of intruding because we're on our honeymoon. Strange how romantic people can become over newly-weds.'

They had seen Urfo and Kirsty off and Sabina had put Kirsty's disturbing figure out of her thoughts as their car had disappeared down the driveway of the villa. The deep timbre of David's voice, his arm loosely encircling her slender shoulders, brought her abruptly back into his world. Now, she thought, I am down to earth once more. How sweet it had been to be caught up for a time in another world, a world in which she had thought to belong with David. She had been touched for a brief time only by the glow between Max and Kirsty. How easily one could be carried away by it, lose one's sense of direction as she had lost hers. Once David and herself had been passionately in love, soaring above earthly spheres. They were now two practical people with important issues at stake and important decisions to make.

David was speaking again. 'Let's stroll down to the lake before we go in,' he said. 'You can tell me what Max said about your knee.'

Sabina suffered the warmth of his encircling arm. 'I pulled a tendon. I have to rest a while and not overdo things.'

She was surprised to discover that she could speak so coolly; all her pulses were hammering at his proximity.

'Then perhaps you will do just that,' he said. 'Has he said any more about the operation on your face?'

'No. It wasn't mentioned. Why?'

'No reason. I just wondered. You might be less edgy when it's done.'

She said testily. 'What would you say was a cure for your edginess?'

'Am I edgy?' David smiled in a way that suggested her question was childish. 'I have a lot on my mind, my sweet. You make your own troubles. Mine are ready-made.'

His arm had moved from her shoulders down to her trim waist, a strong, flexible grasp, entirely impersonal. But the beauty of the evening was changing her mood, an evening of sunlit muted brightness, calm sparkling water, dark blue sky, air so crystal clear that it scintillated like champagne. Several craft were outlined against the sun on the lake. It seemed that all nature's beauty was allied against her on the side of David. The magic of his nearness, the undeniable beauty of his voice, the intentness of his gaze, all were fused together as a whole altogether powerful, compelling, and impossible to resist until the small voice inside her whispered 'Shani'.

'Poor you,' she scoffed, glad that the irregular beat of her heart steadied back to normal.

'It's nothing that I can't handle,' he replied evenly.

Her heart contracted. David had spoken with the confidence of a man who knew his own mind. Held against his strongly built powerful body, Sabina tried to keep her emotions under control. Upon reaching the edge of the lake they stood in silence, gazing across the molten surface as the sun struck it with gold and flame. Sabina thought, we look like lovers, yet we couldn't be more apart.

David said, 'Did you say Kirsty had once been engaged to Max?'

'Yes, I did.'

'Then wasn't it a bit of an anti-climax to ask them both here for the evening?'

'You invited them, I didn't. It was also your fault that

Max came. You insisted upon me seeing a doctor and I chose Max,' she argued.

'So it was my fault. What happened when you girls were alone with him? How did he treat Kirsty? Friendly, was he?'

'Very professional. He told Kirsty that she had fluid under her knee and prescribed pills for her to take.'

There was a pregnant silence. Then David said, softly, dangerously, 'You know, don't you, that we're making conversation like two people waiting for the curtain to go up on a drama which we have to see through to the end. What do you think, my sweet? Will the play have a happy ending or are the leading two miscast?' He looked down at her with a smile that did not reach his eyes. 'Interesting, wouldn't you say?'

Sabina quelled a shiver. His supporting arm was a searing hot brand.

'Come on,' he said abruptly. 'We'd better go in.'

They had reached the staircase when he dropped his arm from her waist and curled strong fingers around her arm.

He said, 'I'll come upstairs with you in case your knee lets you down. How does it feel?'

'Fine.' Her nerves felt at breaking point. There was no anger in the tide of feeling which threatened to choke her, only a kind of choking need for his arm around her again. She pushed her feelings into the background and rested a hand on the balustrade as they walked up the stairs. As they reached the door of their room he looked down at her set face and said curtly,

'Don't worry, I'm not coming to bed yet. I have work to do downstairs. It's possible that I might have to go to Helsinki for a day or so with Urfo and Skip concerning the project we have in hand. You might ask Kirsty to stay with you while I am away, since she will be alone too.'

The next moment he had gone downstairs and Sabina went slowly into the room. So he was going away. The villa would not be the same without him. Nowhere would. She leaned back against the door panels and closed her eyes. How much longer had it to go on—this awful uncertainty? The thought that David might meet Shani in Helsinki stabbed her. She swallowed on the swelling in her throat, tears pricked her eyes. Then she began to prepare for bed. When he eventually came to bed she feigned sleep. He came quite near to the bed, but there was no fleeting touch of his lips or his hand. He moved almost noiselessly across the carpet to his own room.

CHAPTER EIGHT

Sabina gazed unseeingly across the lake waiting for Kirsty to arrive. She had asked her by telephone that morning if she would care to come to spend the day with her. Kirsty had been quite happy to accept the invitation since her brother Urfo was going to Helsinki with David and Skip for an important conference concerning the project they had in hand. They would be away for a few days and Kirsty was doing Urfo's packing.

David had already left. Sabina had gone with him to the door of the villa, where he had given her a hard kiss. Eila and Leif were there to see him go and Sabina felt that the kiss was for their benefit. His lips, cool and firm, had rested upon her own, then he had gone. The memory of it disturbed her and idiotically she lifted a hand as though to feel the imprint on her lips.

There was no getting through to David these last few days at all. He was her husband, yet he was not hers, and he might be seeing Shani every day he was away. And there was nothing she could do about it.

The water was as smooth as cream this morning, but its tranquillity did nothing for her restless mind. She was lost in unhappy thoughts when the sound of a car and the slam of its door alerted her to someone arriving. Was it Kirsty? So soon?

Slowly Sabina turned to walk back to the villa and almost collided with Shani.

'Hello,' the girl greeted her airily. 'I've come for a few things from my room. I hope you don't mind.'

Her dark eyes roved insolently over Sabina's enchanting dress in white cheesecloth with an embroidered yoke.

Sabina returned her gaze with wide-eyed apprehension. Shani had taken her unawares as usual—something she appeared to take a delight in doing.

'Have you come alone?' she asked.

Shani gave a small smile. 'You mean has Bill come with me? No. He has left Helsinki.' Her voice was waspish. 'He was quite taken with you. I don't know why.'

'That makes two of us, since I can't for the life of me see why David should be taken with you.'

Sabina regarded her steadily, noting how the turquoise sun-suit with its bare midriff showed off the tan of her shapely limbs. She was remembering the times when David had regarded girls like Shani with a cool smile of amusement, acknowledging their absurd sexy walk with uplifted cynical brows.

Shani's eyes flashed. 'You will not see anything that you don't want to see. Your marriage is no marriage and you know it.'

Quite calmly Sabina argued, 'How do you know? You met David on a short visit here and now you're claiming him as the one and only love in your young life. I rather think it's you who won't see anything you don't want to see. I know my husband much better than you do. He's the kind of man who having seen something he wants goes after it. He married me because he wanted me.'

'That's what you want to think, isn't it?' Shani tossed her head and stormed. 'You have convinced yourself that David loves you because he married you. Well, I know different. Why do you think I am here? I will tell you. I have come to collect several of my evening dresses. Aunt allows me to go out in the evenings providing I have a suitable escort. I think David is a suitable escort, don't you?'

Sabina winced inwardly and clenched her hands. For sheer effrontery the girl took her breath away.

'You can't convince me that your aunt would approve of a married man taking you out, a man much older than you, and one only recently married.'

Shani gave a triumphant smirk. 'But David is rather special, isn't he? You see, my parents asked him to keep an eye on me while they are away. Naturally you will object since he married you, but he still belongs to me.'

'You talk like a child—really, Shani! David belongs to no one but himself. I don't believe for a moment that your parents did any such thing. You have a nerve, coming here with your fairy tales. Take your dresses and go. I can easily corroborate your story by contacting your parents.'

But Shani was in no way abashed. 'I shall have David in the end, you'll see.'

With this parting shot she marched indoors leaving Sabina trembling and nonplussed. Shani evidently knew about David going to Helsinki—and how did she know unless David had told her? Sabina gave a bewildered sigh. Her blue eyes darkened unhappily as she gazed across the lake. Of one thing she could be sure—if Shani wanted to marry David so much she would do so eventually, providing he was in the same mind about her. Sabina shivered as though an east wind had gone right through to her heart, freezing it for all time. So immersed in her own thoughts was she that she never heard Shani leave. It was a relief to return to the villa some time later to find her gone.

Sabina was crossing the hall when the telephone rang.

It was Max. Could she come to the hospital right away for her operation? A patient whom he was to operate on that day had an infection. He knew it was short notice, but he was sure that she would not mind. Mind! Sabina could not answer for a moment, she was so overcome. It could not have happened at a better time. She had been about at the end of her tether.

Kirsty arrived as she was putting the telephone down. On breath regained, Sabina said, 'Oh, Kirsty, I know you're on your holiday, but will you please take me to the hospital in Helsinki right now? Max is going to operate on my face—isn't it wonderful?'

Kirsty went a little pale. 'I'm so happy for you. Of course I will take you. Come, I will help you pack a few things together. We must get in touch with David.'

'Oh, no, that's the last thing I want,' said Sabina hurriedly. 'He can't do anything and he's at an important conference. Time for him to know later when it's all over.'

'But do you not want him with you at such a time? He will be very upset if he is not told.'

Sabina insisted, 'But, Kirsty, think what a surprise it's going to be for him when the operation is over. You don't know how I've been longing for this day. Now I shall soon know the worst. Max assures me that the operation will be a success, and I have to believe him.' Her face crumpled. 'Oh, Kirsty, I'm so frightened. What if it isn't?'

Kirsty took her arm and marched her towards the stairs. 'You are not to talk like that. Max is a very clever surgeon. Come on, no more nonsense. I'll help you pack a bag.'

Sabina told Eila and Leif that she was spending a day

or so with Kirsty, which was true in a way since Kirsty would be with her at the hospital as much as she would be allowed as a visitor. As Kirsty drove her away from the villa she talked about the beauty of Helsinki, the park high on Observatory hill, the palaces, the market place, the lovely fountains, the Esplanaadikatu with the wide tree-shaded gardens and the statue of Runeberg, the sculptor.

At the hospital Sabina was greeted warmly in reception as a patient of Max and they were conducted to a small ward sparsely furnished but not austere. Max came, flicked a glance at Kirsty and had a few words with Sabina. There was absolutely nothing to worry about, he assured her.

When Kirsty had gone with a promise to come and see her as soon as possible Sabina felt terribly alone. She lay there in the bed with her hands clenched, realising that she was probably quite near to where David was attending his conference. She thought of Shani and her evening dresses, her insolence, her confident assumption that she would soon be with him. Maybe they were right for each other, as Shani had said, and she had been deluding herself. The long years ahead without David were bleak and meaningless if this was true. Tears pricked her eyelids. She had never felt so alone. She thought of Kirsty and hoped that it was not too much of an ordeal for her to come into contact with Max again so soon. The look between them the previous evening had been misinterpreted it seemed. It had been wishful thinking on her part to bring them together.

Sabina's operation was successful, but when Kirsty visited her at the hospital she found a very pale and listless girl with only half her face visible from the bandages around it. She rallied to Kirsty's visit and the news that David had rung to announce that he would be staying with Urfo in Helsinki. She thanked Kirsty for all she had done in covering her tracks to the hospital.

Kirsty said confidently, 'With luck the conference could take a week, so David will be well out of the way while you are recovering, though what he is going to say when he finds out that you have gone through it all alone I cannot imagine.'

Sabina gave a thin smile. 'We shall face that when it's all over. I owe you so much, Kirsty. I feel so overwhelmed by your kindness and Max's that I feel I can never make it up to you.' Tears of weakness came into her eyes as she surveyed the fruit, flowers, sweets and a beautifully illustrated book on the beauty spots of Finland. 'This is lovely,' she ended huskily, picking it up. 'You shouldn't have brought me all this.'

Kirsty said lightly, 'You would have done the same for me. I brought the book for you to browse through because when you are better you will be able to visit all the beauty spots in it.' Her smile was warm as she added, 'Either with me or David. I trust the pain of your operation and other incidents not too pleasant that you have gone through while you have been here will not lessen your fondness for my country.'

Sabina caressed the beautifully illustrated jacket of the book with pale fingers. She knew then that Kirsty had guessed the trouble Shani was causing. Having gone through the same thing herself, she understood.

She noticed that Kirsty seemed to be much on edge, noticed the way she blanched when the door of the private ward opened to admit a nurse with pills for Sabina to take. It did not take much intelligence to see that Kirsty was afraid of Max coming in. Poor Kirsty, she thought, she's still in love with him. If only it was possible to discover if he was still in love with her! The thing was to keep her here as long as possible. But the pills Sabina had taken were already working and her eyelids were drooping.

It was Max who was standing by her bedside when she awoke. He was looking down at her with his charming smile.

'How do you feel?' he asked, placing the back of his fingers on her pale forehead.

'Fine, thanks.' Her wide-set eyes searched his face as she uttered the dreaded question. 'How did it go? Will it be a success? Please tell me the truth, Max!'

She was wide awake now and trembling. So much depended upon his answer, David's future happiness with whoever he wanted and her own peace of mind. Unconsciously one of her trembling hands sought Max's strong firm one and he took it in both his.

'I am sure you will be delighted with the result. You have a healthy constitution and good healing skin. Within a week you will not know yourself.'

He released her hand after giving it a comforting squeeze and turned to the book on the bedside table that Kirsty had bought her.

'I see you have had a visitor this morning,' he said, picking it up and leafing through it. 'From Kirsty,' he added with a lifted brow. 'Not from David, then? You have not let him know yet?'

Sabina bit her lip. 'No. I want it to be a complete surprise. I want to be well and myself again when I see him. I'm afraid I haven't been easy to live with since the accident. I can't tell you how thankful I am that the operation is over, and so thankful to you for all you've done for me, Max. I can never hope to repay you.'

He did not answer right away because he was still looking at the inscription Kirsty had written in the book. When he looked up his eyes had a tired look.

'You can repay me,' he answered, 'by following my instructions and keeping your face fairly static until the skin becomes really attached. When is Kirsty coming again? I wish to see how her knee is progressing.'

'Oh, yes, her knee. I'd forgotten about it, mine too. She really ought to be resting hers instead of coming to see me,' Sabina said with a feeling of guilt.

He smiled. 'A little exercise will not do it any harm and Kirsty comes to see you in her car, so there is not much walking involved. If she happens to come to see you this evening will you tell her that I wish to see her in my office before she leaves?'

'Of course.' Sabina watched him put the book down thoughtfully and added, 'Is it possible for me to contact David by telephone at the conference?'

Max nodded. 'I will see that a telephone is brought in to you.'

When the telephone arrived Sabina sat eyeing it for a long time before plucking up enough courage to use it. When at last she managed it the short interval while David was being contacted at the conference gave her time to steady her voice.

'Hello, David here. Is that you, Sabina?'

His deep voice sent a quiver through her and tears rushed to her eyes as she realised how she had missed him.

'Yes, this is Sabina. How are you, and how is the conference going?'

'As well as can be expected. I'm all right. How are you?'

'I'm beginning to feel much better.'

'Because we're apart or because you hear my voice?'

'It's lovely to hear you, of course.' Sabina's hand holding the receiver was shaking. It would be so easy to tell him where she was and to say how she had missed him, but she had her pride.

'But you're happy that we're apart? Have you seen Max, by the way?'

Her heart dipped. 'Yes, I have. He's very busy at the hospital. My knee is getting better.'

'That's something anyway.' He sounded cynical. 'Look, I must go. Look after yourself. Shall I telephone you this evening?'

She hesitated. 'You can telephone if you like, but we might be out. I'll telephone you in the morning if you like.'

A pause, then, 'As long as you're all right there's no need to worry about telephoning me. This thing will be over in a few days, so I shall come and pick you up when I drop Urfo off at his door. His car will be in dock here until the weekend, so I shall be running him back when the conference ends.'

'I'll be seeing you then.'

A few more words from David and he was gone. As she put down the receiver Sabina felt bruised and battered as if all feeling had gone. They had spoken like mere acquaintances instead of a newly married couple. When Kirsty came that evening Sabina told her what David had said and also gave her the message from Max that he wanted to see her about her knee.

Kirsty coloured, and passed it off by talking about David.

'You will have to ask Max to let you go home in time, then David can pick you up from our house. I do not see why you should not if I promise him to look after you,' she reasoned.

Sabina looked hopeful. 'Do you think Max would?'

'I will ask him when I see him. My knee is much better. The swelling has gone. The pills he gave me did the trick, and the rest, I suppose.'

Sabina said, 'Max was looking at your book this morning and he gazed for some time on the inscription you'd written inside. I thought he was looking rather tired.'

'What did he say about your face? Not that I have any doubt that it will not be a perfect job. Max is a perfectionist in his work.'

'I think he's marvellous,' agreed Sabina. 'He must have heaps of girls falling over themselves for him to notice them. He's fairly confident about the result. I could have kissed him when he told me, but instead I hung on to his hand near to tears.'

She laughed and waited for Kirsty to show some sign of her feelings for Max, but her expression did not alter.

'There is one thing about Max that I admire very much,' Sabina went on. 'He's not a philanderer. He has always instilled in me a feeling of trust. I'm sure he'll make some lucky girl an excellent husband.'

Kirsty smiled. 'You are very sweet, Sabina, but if you are trying to bring Max and me together you are wasting your time. His mother would fight me tooth and nail if I went anywhere near him.'

Kirsty had lost colour. Her eyes were dark with unhappy memories and Sabina's heart went out to her.

She said, 'Having met Anna Hiltunsen I'm not surprised. But surely you love Max enough to fight for him.

I would, mother or no mother. Besides, you have Max on your side.'

Sadly Kirsty shook her head. 'I have no wish to come between them. Max is very proud and fond of his mother, so things are better left as they are.' She smiled wistfully. 'The trouble is that he has spoiled me for any other man.'

Sabina said, 'David has done that for me too. I know how you feel. But are you doing the right thing in giving up so easily?'

Kirsty shrugged. 'One has to get over these things. I shall in time. I simply could not go through it all again.'

When Kirsty had gone Sabina lay thinking over what she had said about fighting for Max. The joke was on herself in telling Kirsty to do something she was not prepared to do herself, fight for her own husband.

CHAPTER NINE

SABINA'S stay in hospital would have been almost enjoyable, for the staff were kind and considerate, the meals were good and the operation on her face did not curtail any pleasures like moving about freely or reading. But for the fact that the fear of David finding out about her being there was always present, she was almost happy.

It was a relief therefore when she eventually moved to Kirsty's house. She had been careful to telephone David every morning from the hospital and no matter how she had tried her remarks to him had always been somewhat stilted. His replies had not been much better. Sabina had experienced the feeling of talking to him through a thick fog of misunderstanding and fear, fear that they were going further and further away from each other. He had not mentioned calling at Kirsty's house to see her again, also he had stayed in town instead of returning to their own villa each evening as he had done during the first part of his stay in Helsinki.

On Friday morning Sabina telephoned him from the villa and this time she endeavoured to keep the relief that she was out of the hospital from her voice. But she must have sounded quite different to David, because he replied on a surprised note.

'You sound different this morning,' he said. 'Do I detect a note of happiness in your voice? Was the break from me something you needed after all?'

'Maybe we both needed the break,' she replied. 'I've missed you, David.'

She held her breath as she waited for his reply. It was a long time in coming and it was in jocular vein.

'For a girl on her honeymoon to say that to her husband must be the understatement of the year! I shall be home tomorrow and I'll pick you up.' A pause. 'I don't suppose Kirsty would drive you into Helsinki and we could swop passengers? Urfo's car is in dock here and I'm bringing him back to his house.'

Sabina's hand moved protectively to the dressing on her cheek at his words. She could not spring the surprise of her operation on him in the presence of Urfo and Kirsty. She had to see his honest reaction, not one put on for the benefit of their friends. The sound of his voice had set her heart surging with joy and the longing to see him again was overwhelming.

'Are you still there?'

His deep voice cut in on her bewildered thoughts, and she broke into a cold sweat. How easy it would be to tell him about the operation, tell him how she loved him, and how she had missed him. But she had to see the expression on his face when she told him.

'Yes,' she replied, 'I'm still here. I hope you don't mind, but I'd rather you came to collect me from Kirsty's house.'

David sounded easy. 'All right, my sweet, if that's what you want. I had a notion that perhaps we could stay in Helsinki for a day or two and I could show you the sights. However, I forgot how sensitive you are about your face. See you soon. Take care.'

Sabina replaced the receiver with a trembling hand. Her eyes misted with tears, but she brushed them away quickly at the sound of Kirsty's voice. Then she appeared in the doorway with a slender boyish figure beside her and Sabina ran forward to fling herself into his arms.

'Blair!' she cried. 'Why didn't you tell me you were coming?' The tears came anew to her eyes as she hugged him.

'Tears?' he mocked. 'Not for me, surely?'

He gave her his handkerchief, and she dabbed her eyes.

'And what, my dear brother, are you doing here?' she asked with a fond smile.

'A photographic assignment in Helsinki for a few days. I arrived yesterday,' he answered with a grin. Suddenly his eyes were on the dressing on her cheek. 'Say, they haven't done your scar, have they?'

Sabina nodded happily. 'Isn't it wonderful?'

'Great,' he replied. 'Does that mean you'll do some part-time modelling for me when you get back home?' He squeezed her arm. 'I suppose you'll still be pie-eyed over the guy when you return home from your honeymoon. Where is David, by the way?'

'In Helsinki at a conference. He's coming to pick me up tomorrow to take me back to the villa. How did you know I was here?'

'A nice couple at your villa told me where I could find you. They said nothing about your operation.'

She said hastily, 'They didn't know about it. Neither does David. He went away for a week and they sent for me at the hospital quite unexpectedly. David was busy and . . .'

Sabina broke off lamely at the surprise on his face. 'You mean he doesn't know you've been in hospital? You never told him?'

'That's right. It's going to be a surprise. That's why I'm staying here with Kirsty. Kirsty is a nurse.'

'You mean the girl who let me in, with the smashing dark eyes?' Blair grinned. 'She's photogenic if anyone was. I'd love to take some photographs of her.'

'I'll introduce you.' Sabina, seeing that Kirsty had left them together, linked his arm and walked with him from the hall to the lounge. Seeing her beloved brother again had done much for her morale. They had always been close and her own troubles vanished in thin air in his company. Besides, a little plan was forming in her mind, a plan which brought a smile to her face.

'Blair,' she said thoughtfully, 'Max Hiltunsen, the surgeon who has operated on my face, is calling this morning, and I want you to be very nice to Kirsty when he arrives. Make a fuss of her, let Max see that you admire her. Will you do that?'

Blair flung himself into a chair and looked up at her warily. 'Max Hiltunsen?' he replied with a wrinkled brow. 'Isn't he that big handsome chap who patched you up after your accident? Are he and Kirsty connected in some way?' He grinned. 'You'd better tell me more before I commit myself. Max is some man.'

Sabina laughed. 'Max is a wonderful person and so is Kirsty. He's also gentle and kind, but that's all I'm telling you at the moment. I'm asking a special favour of you and I know you won't let me down.'

Before Blair could answer Kirsty appeared in the doorway. Her face looked strained.

She said, 'I have just heard a car arriving. I think it is Max, so I will leave you with him.'

'No, don't go,' Sabina cried as she was about to leave the room. 'I want to introduce you to my brother Blair. Blair, this is my friend Kirsty Mikkola. Her brother Urfo is a colleague of David's on his present project.'

Blair got to his feet and took Kirsty's hand to hold on to it as he acknowledged the introduction.

'I've just been telling Sabby here what beautiful eyes you have. I'm a professional photographer, Kirsty, and I would very much like to take some photographs of you. Did you know you have a photogenic face?'

'I have?' Kirsty blushed and raised slim fingers to her hot cheek. She was too overcome by Blair's audacious praise to be aware of the big figure filling the doorway. 'You are teasing me, of course.'

'No, I mean it. Ever thought of being a model? I see you have no ring.' Blair looked at the slim fingers clasped in his hands which he was holding on to for the benefit of Max standing glaring in the doorway. 'I'm perfectly respectable,' Blair went on. 'Sabby used to model for me before she was married. With your face and those long legs you're just the kind of replacement I've been looking for.'

'I suppose it is all right if I come in?' Max put in suavely. 'The door was open and no one was about.'

He strolled in looking well-groomed in a grey suit and a pale blue shirt which brought out the gold in his hair. His smile included them all and Blair was in no way put out. Against the tall wide-shouldered figure of Max, he looked very young and slender, but his cream safari suit was just as elegant as the older man's. Releasing Kirsty's hands, he greeted the newcomer cordially.

'I'm glad to meet you, sir,' he said. 'I saw you once in London, but I don't suppose you'll remember me. I'm Blair Farne, Sabina's brother, and I would like to take this opportunity to thank you for all you've done for her. I'm very, very grateful.'

Max smiled, and shook his hand. 'I believe you are

making quite a reputation in your work. I also have a job of work which, like you, I try to do to the best of my ability. However, I have not much time, so if you will excuse me . . .'

With hardly a glance at Kirsty, Max approached Sabina to examine her face. His examination was brief but thorough and he gave her a satisfied smile.

'The skin is knitting together beautifully,' he said, smearing on the special cream he used. 'How do you feel?'

'Wonderful now that it's all over,' Sabina sighed.

She was vaguely aware of Kirsty pressing Blair to stay for the midday meal and then leaving the room to go to the kitchen. Sabina guessed that Kirsty would be thankful that the housekeeper was away since it gave her an excuse to avoid Max.

As for Max, there was no way of telling how he had taken the little scene of Blair holding Kirsty's hand and regarding her with blatant admiration while he paid her outrageous compliments. Sabina could only hope that her plan would bear fruit. Max left without Kirsty putting in an appearance and Sabina went to the kitchen to help her to prepare the lunch.

Both girls enjoyed Blair's company and the afternoon was spent with him taking photographs of Kirsty. Sabina refused to have her picture taken even with the good side of her face, which was proving beyond all her hopes to be no more perfect than the other when it had healed.

She had lost a little weight under the strain, but the hollow-cheeked look was both lovely and enchanting. It added a poignant beauty to her wide-spaced blue eyes and Blair was most enthusiastic about it.

'You've changed, Sabby,' he said as they lazed on the

terrace that afternoon. 'You've grown into a real beauty with that high-cheekboned little-girl-lost look. My pictures are going to make you the most sought-after model in the U.K. In you and Kirsty I have the best of both worlds, a stunning blonde and brunette.'

Kirsty had gone to the kitchen to fetch them a cool drink and Sabina laughed at his enthusiasm.

'Don't count your chickens,' she teased. 'I'm a married woman, and Kirsty could be soon.'

But even as she spoke the words Sabina knew that both statements were wishful thinking. She was not sure of David and Kirsty was not sure of Max. But at least along with Kirsty she had the chance of a great career working with Blair. Yet the thought of it brought no joy. All she wanted was to be David's wife and the mother of his children, just as she was sure Kirsty did with Max. It would not be long now before she found out where David's love was. Now that her face was well on the way to recovering its former smoothness of skin with no scars to mar it, he could annul their marriage with impunity if he so wished. As the time drew nearer for his return she began to grow more nervous. She had to arrange his arrival to coincide with her being in her room in order to see his reaction. Not that she would be able to read much from it, but it might open the door for further discussion.

Blair had gone back to his hotel in Helsinki in the car he had rented from a garage there, and she had settled down to a quiet evening with Kirsty. Urfo called on the telephone around nine o'clock to tell Kirsty that he would be home the following morning. The conference had gone well and everything was satisfactory. David was out, he had no idea where. A telephone call had come for him and he had gone out about an hour earlier. He would probably telephone when he arrived back at the hotel.

Kirsty passed on the conversation to Sabina, who went ice-cold on being told about David. It could not be Blair who had telephoned him since he had no idea where he was in Helsinki and he had also been aware of the need for secrecy which Sabina wanted in order to surprise him over her operation. It could only be Shani who had contacted him. No doubt he had spent his last evening with her before returning to the villa the next morning. Later, in her room, Sabina sat until midnight waiting for David to get in touch with her since Urfo was sure to tell him of the telephone call he had made to Kirsty. But no call came.

She was dead tired but beyond sleep when at last she crawled into bed to shiver, not from cold but from some kind of premonition.

She awoke the next morning unrefreshed and with a head heavy as lead. The pretty room Kirsty had given her looked no different, but its friendliness did nothing to touch her troubled heart that seemed to have gone into cold storage. Her expression as she looked at herself in the dressing-table mirror was deadpan. There were tired circles under her eyes and the skin looked yellow around the dressing on her cheek. For all she cared the scar could still be there.

As she bathed and dressed, Sabina knew that she had been hopelessly illogical. David had married her and all she had done was to repulse him and send him into Shani's arms. Why then was she worrying about his affair with Shani? Would not Shani make him happier than she had done? She had shut him out of her life and he had gone to someone else—it was as simple as that.

Kirsty came to bring her an early morning drink, enquired about her face, had a look at it and nodded with satisfaction. She sat on Sabina's bed looking very pretty in a leaf green housecoat which went with her russet hair. Since Blair's visit the previous day she had appeared to bloom like a girl who had found a new slant on life.

'I have been thinking, Sabina,' she admitted almost reluctantly. 'Your brother Blair has been painting a very attractive picture of life as a photographer's model. Perhaps you can tell me something about it. You see, I was considering leaving the country and trying something abroad.' She gave a small somewhat cynical laugh. 'I never imagined I had the kind of looks suitable for that kind of life. You, yes, but not me.'

Sabina snorted. 'I'm no beauty. I happened to be photogenic like you. Lots of models aren't beautiful, they just happen to have the right kind of features that look well when photographed. If you're worried in case Blair is kidding you—by that I mean acting the fool—I can assure you that he isn't. You lived too long in the shadow of Mrs Hiltunsen to be aware of your own attractiveness.'

Sabina found herself speaking the truth about Blair. He was essentially honest, but he had gone a bit too far in trying to entice Kirsty away when she wanted to keep her there for Max. Something stubborn in Sabina's nature insisted that she was not wrong about Kirsty and Max. They still loved each other. It was unthinkable that Kirsty and herself would be leaving the country minus David and Max.

Kirsty smiled. 'That is very sweet of you, Sabina. You are very good for my morale, but I am going away. Urfo is all right with his housekeeper and it will do me good to travel for a while. I have some money of my own.'

Sabina finished her drink. 'Thanks, Kirsty, that was nice. You know, I can't see you travelling alone through life. You aren't the career kind, you're much too sentimental and gentle. Modelling is nothing to run after, not compared with marrying some nice man and settling down with a family.'

Kirsty rose to her feet as if to end the conversation. She said, 'See you at breakfast. Did Max say whether he was coming today?'

She bent her head to pick up the tray, but Sabina saw, her lip tremble.

'No. There is one thing. If Blair calls this morning before David, I shall ask him to take me back to the Villa. I would like to be there when David returns.'

Kirsty looked up in surprise. 'If you really want to go Sabina, I will take you,' she said. 'We can leave a note for David. I suppose you told Max you would not be here?'

'No. I didn't. His own place is near to here so he will probably call on his way home.'

Kirsty went pale at the thought. 'You could telephone him at the hospital,' she suggested.

Sabina teetered on seeing the worried frown on her face. 'All right. I will do just that. When do we start? After breakfast?'

Kirsty was quiet during the drive back to the Villa and Sabina had never felt less like talking. A faint weight of depression was weighing her down as they reached the door and Eila stood there with Leif having heard the car.

Eila's exclamation on seeing Sabina's face as she left the car was one of surprise and delight.

'You have had your face done?' she cried. 'Now I see why you were so anxious to have the operation. Even with a dressing on it your face looks different. You are lovely is she not Leif?'

Eila turned to her husband for confirmation of her words and he nodded shyly.

'Very beautiful indeed,' he replied.

'Thank you.' Sabina would not have been human if she had not been flattered at their praise and she felt her depression lift. If only David would react in the same way after her keeping the operation a secret from him!

With this in mind, she said quickly, 'My husband doesn't know I've had the operation. I want it to be a surprise when he comes later today.'

Eila and Leif nodded in agreement and went indoors, Leif carrying Sabina's suitcase. Then Kirsty wound down the window of her car.

'I am driving back now if it is all right with you, Sabina. With David home you will not be wanting to see me again and soon I have to return to work.'

Sabina looked down at her fondly. 'I shall never be able to thank you, Kirsty, for what you've done for me. I would like you to come and visit us often here at the villa. Blair is coming to stay with us for a day or so and he will want to see you too.'

Kirsty smiled. 'He is nice, your brother. I want you to give him a message for me if you will. Will you tell him that I have made up my mind to go with him to England and be a model. I shall have to give in my notice at the hospital.'

For a moment Sabina stared at her aghast. 'Are you sure that's what you want, Kirsty?' she asked. 'There's nothing to keep you here?'

Kirsty shook her head. She looked pale, tight-lipped. 'No, nothing. I ought to have left long ago. Do you know,' a pale little smile, 'now I have made my mind up I already begin to feel better.'

It was on the tip of Sabina's tongue to tell her that she did not look better, she looked awful. Her eyes were shadowed as if she had not been sleeping, and she looked almost numb. She had spoken with the calm, steady assurance of one who was taking the only way out of trouble that had dogged her far too long.

Sabina was torn by conflicting emotions. For all she knew she might be going back with Kirsty herself. Like Kirsty's affair with Max, her marriage seemed to have everything against it. She and David were like two people marking time until the last act in their drama was played out to the inevitable end.

'Yes, I'll tell Blair what you've decided,' she said. 'He'll be delighted.'

And now to meet David, Sabina thought as Kirsty disappeared in her car. The time dragged. She had gone to her room, emptied her suitcase, separated those things to be laundered from others which she placed in her wardrobe, and had wandered into David's dressing room. The divan was not made up into a bed, his dressing robe had gone and his set of brushes from the tallboy. She wondered if he had used the double bed in which she had slept on the nights he had returned to sleep at the villa, and if he had been haunted by her.

Sabina felt a chill of fear that she might have lost David's love, or worse still, had never really had it. Well, she would soon know. Nervously she brushed her hair. Strange that she should feel so little reaction to her operation now that it was all over. There would be no more subterfuge, no more sensitive furtive movements in efforts to camouflage its existence, no more painful reactions to people's curious stares. But most of all no more shrinking from David's lips.

She could not wait for him to arrive and when a car broke the silence as it fast approached the villa, she ran downstairs to meet him. But it was not David, it was Max.

The high-powered car stood gleaming in the sun looking no less colossal than the man himself as he unwound his big frame from the interior.

'You don't mind me coming back to the villa, do you, Max?' she asked anxiously.

'Not at all. You are on your honeymoon and I have parted you and David for long enough. In any case, your skin is healing so well that I could very well have missed today seeing you.' He smiled, examined her cheek and feathered strong fingers, light and gentle as a breeze, over the dressing. 'Beautiful,' he told Sabina appreciatively, touching the skin graft as if he loved it.

'I still can't believe it's all over,' she said, walking indoors with him. 'I'm so grateful to you for doing it for me. I know how you must be pushed for time, but you've never grudged me a moment, not even when I've barged in on your leisure.'

'Why should I? You have been one of my favourite cases. And shall I tell you something?' He smiled down at her, his eyes twinkling, and Sabina thought how very attractive he was. 'When I operated upon your face I knew that there would be no complications.'

'Ouch!' she cried with a pout. 'And I was thinking you'd been bowled over by my feminine charms.'

'Careful now,' he teased. 'I am only a man but

fortunately I am a doctor first. Come on, I will renew the dressing, then I must go before David throws me out.'

'But David isn't here yet. Kirsty brought me over. Have you seen her?'

'No. I received your message at the hospital. Where is Kirsty?'

There was nothing in his manner to show that he felt more than a casual interest in her friend, and Sabina could have shaken him.

Baldly, she said, 'Did you know that my brother has offered her a job as photographic model? She's planning on leaving the hospital and the country.'

'Is that so?'

Max said no more, but she thought he was unusually quick dressing her cheek. But his next words dashed all her hopes.

'I am to meet Mother in Helsinki to bring her home from her visit to friends when I leave here,' he volunteered. 'There, how does it feel? Comfortable? Nice when you can dispense with dressings and leave the skin to heal in the fresh air. Now it is beginning to look better.'

He turned her to look into a mirror and she stared at the skin healing miraculously over what had once been a scar. But all she could think about was poor Kirsty eating her heart out for him.

'You are very quiet,' he commented. 'Does it not meet with your approval?'

'Oh, goodness, yes. It's wonderful, and I love you!' she cried.

Sabina was not quite herself in that moment, for she flung her arms around his neck and reached up to kiss him soundly. Maybe she had some wild idea of hanging on to him to stop him from going to meet his mother, since Mrs Hiltunsen's return meant curtains for Kirsty where he was concerned. Whatever it was made her laugh and cry at the same time.

They both turned instinctively to see David in the doorway. Keen-eyed, sunburned, with his dark hair echoing in the darkening of his look, he greeted them coolly.

'Am I interrupting something?' he asked with chilly politeness.

'Of course not,' Sabina said with dignity, although her heart was hammering against her ribs.

He kissed her briefly, conscious, as she was, of Max. As he straightened again she saw that he was not amused. But he strode forward with a smile to greet Max.

'How are you, Max?' he said, and shook his hand.

They exchanged a few banal remarks, then Max had gone. By now Sabina was trembling. It was hardly the welcome she had planned for David, in another man's arms. And there had been more than mere annoyance in his manner at the sight of them both in an embrace. He had not even noticed that her scar had gone.

'How long has Max been here?' he asked in tones distant and remote.

'About ten minutes,' she answered.

'Was that the end of a long greeting I witnessed just now?' His voice was rough and she noticed the tired lines around his eyes for the first time. He had always been so full of energy and to see him like this, tired and dispirited, hurt like a physical pain.

'Max was here to dress my face—in case you haven't noticed.'

The expressions flitted across his face, surprise, anger, and then anxiety. He drew nearer and spoke in tones so controlled that Sabina wondered if she had imagined his various expressions. Gently he took hold of her chin and turned her face upwards to the light.

'So it's all over,' he said softly. 'Was it very painful, the operation?'

His smile was warm, his eyes very gentle with no mockery in them. Sabina felt the blood rush to her face as she became lost in his penetrating look and the beauty of his voice. Oh, David, her heart cried, be nice to me!

She shook her head and he gazed down for a long time into the lovely eyes glistening with unshed tears, the dark gold aura of hair around her head and the tremulous lips.

'I wanted it to be a surprise,' she whispered. 'Are you happy that it's all over? No more moaning from yours truly. I've been pretty awful, haven't I, but I'll make it up to you.'

He kissed her quivering lips, lightly, carelessly. 'Will you? Can you turn back the clock to capture time we've lost? I doubt it.'

That awful barrier had dropped again between them. David was as cold and unapproachable as an iceberg. It's strange, Sabina thought, that I can be so calm at one of the most crucial moments of my life. I've been living with it, though, for some time, waiting for it to come, inevitably, nearer and nearer.

Her voice sounded strange and husky and not hers at all. 'I have so much to tell you, David.'

'That makes two of us. But not now—I have to go out again.' He caught her arm. 'Come with me to our rooms.'

He piloted her upstairs and Sabina looked at his set profile in bewilderment.

'But you've only just come in,' she protested. 'And you haven't said a word about my face.'

He closed the door of their room behind him and leaned back against it to look dispassionately at her face. His finger was hard beneath her chin as she stood there quiveringly and at a loss.

'Max has done a wonderful job,' he told her in a voice without much expression. 'You're lovely, Sabina, do you know that? Far lovelier than you were before, because you're growing up. But I doubt even now whether we speak the same language, you and I. However, we'll come back to that later. Right now I'm with you all the way. I know how you feel, a bit numb that the miracle has happened to make you feel sane and whole again. Suddenly this awful thing that threatened your peace of mind has gone and you're free of it at last. It meant more to you than your husband, your marriage, or anything we could have built up together.' He lifted a hand as she was about to speak. 'No, let me finish. Now that this most important thing in your life has lost all its importance perhaps you'll dwell upon other things—like our marriage.'

He moved away from the door to stride across the room. 'If you'll excuse me, I have to change into a clean shirt.'

He left the door of his dressing room open while he changed into a lounge suit and put on a clean shirt. Then he came striding out to the bedroom, raking back the dark unruly hair from his set face with his fingers.

'Have you a comb?' he asked. 'I've left mine in the car along with my suitcase.'

Sabina gestured to the dressing table and sat down helplessly on the bed. She was trembling, then suddenly she was sitting rigid, her face pale and drawn.

'Might I ask where you're going?' she said weakly.

'I'm going to the hospital,' he said, combing his hair crisply. 'Shani has been in a car accident. She's unconscious, so I'm going to sit by her until she recovers.' He straightened from combing his hair and looking into the dressing table mirror. Then he tapped his pockets for his wallet, passport and other personal belongings. 'I shan't be back tonight in any case.'

It seemed to Sabina that he could not bear to look at her as he went on. 'Shani is not deeply unconscious. Among other things she keeps saying my name, so I'm obliged to sit beside her until she recovers.'

A pulse suddenly made itself felt in the base of Sabina's throat beating like a drum. Her head throbbed with disillusionment, anger, and pain. Their marriage was over, over. Fate had taken a hand by making the blow short and precise. For one wild moment she wanted to run and fling herself into his arms, to bring back to his eyes the searching tenderness which would tell her that all was well between them. But she checked the impulse. Instead she said quite coolly with a calmness that amazed her,

'Shouldn't her parents be the ones to be with her? Have you let them know?'

'No, I haven't. I have my reasons.'

She swallowed on a dry throat. 'But surely her parents should be the first to know? They have a right to be there, more right than . . . than a . . . a lover or anyone else, surely?'

David said stubbornly, 'I'm doing this my way,' as if that explained everything. 'I want you to say nothing about Shani's accident to Eila or anyone. I'm handling the situation myself. Everything is going to be all right, believe me. I know it's rather a lot to ask of you since you never put your trust in me in any case, but this happens to mean a lot to me. Will you do as I ask?'

'Why should I?' she cried. 'It isn't as though you were a single man. You're married, David. Can't you see, or don't you want to? Is this the way out you've been looking for? I implore you to be honest. Are you walking out on me now?'

His mouth thinned. 'You never have trusted me, have you, much less loved me. There's no time to talk now. While I'm away you might think over the position we're in. Even you must see that we can't go on like this.'

He seemed to fling himself out of the room, and Sabina lifted a shaking hand to cover her face. He could not go like that, she thought wildly. There was so much to say. But he had gone, to Shani. In the midst of her own misery she found herself sparing a thought for the girl who had taken everything from her. How ill was she? Would she die? If she did then David might come back to her, give her another chance. But she did not want him that way. He had gone.

Sabina lay down on the bed with her good cheek resting on her arm, but the tears did not come. The hurt had gone beyond them. She wished she was dead.

CHAPTER TEN

How Sabina lived through the rest of the day when David had gone, she never knew. She rested in her room and Eila brought up her meals, seeing nothing out of the ordinary in her resting until her face was healed. She took it for granted that David had gone once more to his work, but her sympathy was with Sabina. Poor child, she had been through so much. Eila was glad her brother had come to cheer her up a bit.

But Blair did not come that day. Late that evening he telephoned Sabina to say that he would not be coming until the following day because he had several important assignments before he was free. She told him about Kirsty's decision to accept his offer of a job as a model and he was delighted. She thought of Max with his mother, by now in Helsinki or on their way home. Everyone seemed to have a goal in life except herself. Well, she had to make one now, one without David. The awful thing was the waiting. She had to wait for her face to heal properly, to finish the treatment, then she could go away.

Max called the next morning and was pleased to see how well the skin graft was going. He enquired how she was feeling and frowned at the dark shadows beneath her eyes.

'Are you not sleeping?' he asked with professional concern. 'You have no pain?'

'No. I must be suffering from a kind of anti-climax. I

can't believe I've lost my scar for good,' she said.

He said thoughtfully as though not entirely convinced, 'I expected a far different reaction from you. Where is David?'

The question took her unawares and she strove for calm. 'He's out,' she replied inadequately. 'Did you know that Shani Somers is in hospital after a car accident?'

'Yes. She is being discharged this morning, I believe.' He closed the case he had brought with him containing dressings. 'I gather that your husband was at the hospital yesterday.'

Sabina's throat went suddenly dry. She willed a smile to stiff lips.

'David said she was asking for him. He went again to see her last night.'

He nodded thoughtfully, then gave her a reassuring smile. 'No doubt he feels responsible for her with her parents being away. Give him my congratulations, will you, on winning the contract for the job he and his colleagues were after. I hope you both enjoy your prolonged honeymoon.'

'Prolonged honeymoon?' She managed a smile.

'David has at least three months before the project can get under way, so what better than spending it here? I am sure that is what he will do. Another week and your face will be as good as new, then no more feelings of embarrassment for you.'

Sabina laughed. 'I see what you mean. Thanks to you, Max,' she said warmly. 'I'll see you to your car.'

When he had gone she strolled slowly to the lake where she stood staring across the water with unseeing eyes. David had told her nothing about the conference or the time he would have before his contract began. Where was he now? Waiting to escort Shani back to her aunt? But surely her aunt had been at the hospital if what David had said was true about the girl being delirious? But if she was delirious last night what were they doing discharging her this morning?

Sabina pushed the heavy gold hair away from her hot brow and felt hammers going in her temples. The air was warm, the sun blinding and she felt a headache which threatened to blind her with pain. It had been impossible to ask Max for further information about Shani's accident without revealing the rift between herself and David.

She looked at her wristwatch. Not long now to the midday meal, and she did not feel up to eating anything. Maybe a short rest in her room would brighten her up. It would never do for Blair to arrive and find her looking as washed out as she felt. She would have to behave normally while he was here. She would not be staying long herself once her face had healed. If Blair stopped at the villa for a while it would be possible for her to go back with him. David would have surely shown his hand by then. It was up to him to make the next move.

Wearily Sabina went to her room and lay on her bed, wondering what Eila and Leif thought about David going out again last evening and staying out all night. Since David had not told them about Shani's accident they did not know the reason for his absence. They were not stupid and it would not be long before they guessed that something was sadly wrong between their two guests at the villa.

Emptying her mind of all confused thoughts, Sabina lay quiet and relaxed until the headache had gone. It had only been tension that had brought it on. She combed her hair and made herself presentable. If Blair had not arrived she would have to dine alone; it was not likely that David would show up. He might have telephoned. In the mirror her face stared back at her pale and pinched. But the skin around the skin graft on her cheek looked healthy enough.

Blair turned up as Sabina was about to sit down for her midday meal. He was more than ready for his. His battered suitcase had been taken to a guest room by Leif and while he ate he told Sabina about the hectic time he had gone through the previous day. Passing his cup for a second drink of coffee, he said casually, 'The strangest thing happened yesterday.' He paused and looked around the room. 'By the way, where's David?'

Sabina made a vague gesture to flex a trembling hand and tried to speak lightly.

'Out again, I'm afraid. But I believe everything has gone smoothly for him regarding the project he's on. He'll have a few months to relax while it gets under way.'

'That's good news. Sure I won't be in the way here? It'll be great to laze around for a day or so.' He grinned. 'And I promise not to get under your feet.'

Sabina gave him a tender look. 'You know you'll always be welcome, you idiot, wherever I happen to be. You were saying?' she prompted with a vague sense of premonition as she refilled his cup.

'Thanks.' Blair stirred his coffee. 'Oh, yes, where was I? I remember. Among my many activities yesterday I drove a guest to the airport. He was late, couldn't get a taxi, and I happened to be going in that direction. The airport was busy with visitors coming and going and I could have sworn I saw David. Only it couldn't have been him because he was with this girl, a rather attractive girl, who was hanging on to his arm as he carried a huge suitcase. They were hurrying to catch a plane.'

It seemed to Sabina as she listened that the room was playing tricks. Everything was swaying around her. Dew gathered on her temples and she wanted to be sick. She grabbed her cup of coffee and forced some down her throat with trembling hands. It went down the wrong way and she began to choke with coughing.

The next moment Blair was on his feet, taking the cup from her and mopping up the spilled coffee on her dress. Then she was burying her face in his handkerchief as her spluttering gradually ceased.

'All right now?' Blair hovered over her in concern. 'That was quite a turn,' he sympathised.

She mopped streaming eyes, aware that the tears were not all on account of the choking. But the incident, though very unpleasant, had given her time to pull herself together. So David had gone. It was all over, and no amount of tears, wishful thinking, would bring him back. That it was David at the airport with Shani there was no doubt. It explained why she had not heard from him. Next would be a letter from his solicitors. She had never thought David to be a coward, yet he had gone away because he had not the courage to tell her the truth.

It was a knowledge that hurt bitterly. Perhaps, she thought, I deserve to be hurt. The immediate reaction after weeks of sustained emotion culminating in her operation, and now his departure from her life, gave her a sense of unreality. For the time being it was impossible to take in the fact that David had gone, that she would never actually be his wife in the real sense of the word. The success of her operation, something she had been hoping and praying for, had broken the last frail hold she had on him.

Blair was saying, 'You look awfully shaken up. Why not rest upstairs in your room? You'll have to change your dress quickly or the coffee stains won't come out so easily. I have some pictures to develop which will take me until late afternoon. Will it be all right if I use the sauna to do them? I can black it out for the purpose more easily.'

Sabina nodded and looked down vaguely at the coffee stain on her dress. It had obviously gone through to her pretty underwear, but the fact did not dismay her. She was numb.

'Do what you like,' she said. 'Eila and Leif will help you if there's anything you want.'

In her room, Sabina stripped off, put the clothes to soak in cold water in the bathroom, and lay on the bed in her negligee. She lay for a long time with her blue eyes fixed glassily in front of her. Then she closed them as though by doing so she could shut out everything that had happened during the past week or so. The room was very quiet with only the faint ticking of the travelling clock beside the bed.

The sound of a car arriving awakened her. Bemusedly she rose from the bed and drifted to the window, but there was only Blair's rakish-looking hired car that she could see. She must be crazy to think that David would be coming back. It was probably Max come to dress her face. Good heavens, she had nothing on under the wrap. But before she could do anything about it the door opened and someone strode in.

Every scrap of colour left her face. Her blue eyes looked huge and luminous. Her lips were tremulous.

'David!' she whispered in husky tones.

'Yes, David,' he echoed, leaning back against the

closed door in a gesture of weariness. 'Thank God I'm back!'

For a moment Sabina stood tense. She quivered. Her cheeks were rapidly becoming a warm smooth rose. The sun picked the gold in her hair dishevelled as it was curling round her flushed and happy face. The next moment she had flung herself in his arms. All her slim suppleness was pressed against him, bringing the deep fragrance of her hair against his lips, followed by the salt of her happy tears.

She was clinging to him with her arms clasped around his neck. Her face was raised to his and silently, very gently, he was kissing it. His arms were iron bands as their kisses mingled with the salt of her tears. All her sweetness was his, as she clung to him, close, fierce and loving.

Slowly he kissed her soft palpitating throat, her eyes bright with tears, and moved his lips gently around the dressing on her cheek. There was no shrinking on his part from her poor cheek. How could she ever have thought that there would be? She never questioned the miracle that had brought him back to her. He was here, and whatever followed in the future would not dim these moments stolen from time that could never be quite the same again.

His mouth found hers again. They stood as one locked together as they savoured long-denied moments of ecstasy. Everything was forgotten in their need for each other. At last David lifted his head for them both to draw breath.

'That was some welcome!' He gave her a mocking tender appraisal, then kissed her eyelids, her mouth and her soft throat. His hands moved caressingly over her back and he murmured, 'You feel so delicate. Have you nothing on beneath this thing?'

Shamelessly she admitted that this was so, whereupon he chuckled, swept her up into his arms and laid her down upon the bed to lie beside her. She thought, Just because I know nothing about his return here and why he's come I have to be very careful. But I must tell him why I've behaved as I have done. I must explain before I ask him anything.

He had drawn her into his arms. His mouth was again on hers, his hand moving down into the loose collar of her negligee. She caught his hand and he lifted his head.

'Please, David,' she pleaded, 'don't touch me for a moment. I have something to confess. I've always loved you as deeply as I thought you loved me. It . . . it was the scar. I . . . I couldn't bear the thought of being like we are now, in each other's embrace, and you shrinking when your lips happened to touch my scarred cheek. I know now that I was very silly. I do love you, David, really I do. You know something?' Her lovely eyes glistened with tears. 'If I had to choose between having my scar removed and having you, I'd choose you every time.'

He listened while looking at her intently. 'Of all the lovely idiots!' he mocked. 'I'd give you the first prize— me, or rather what's left of me after getting that little wretch Shani Somers off my back. I shall have to begin at the beginning. Comfortable?'

He drew her back into his arms and rested his chin on her hair.

'I suppose it all began on my first visit here. She seemed to take an instant liking to me. I treated her for what she was—a teenager growing up who wanted to know all the answers to being an adult. I never thought for a moment that she could be as devious as she was. She did everything in her power to make me treat her as some fascinating female out for an affair. She was so painfully blatant that I was, more often than not, moved into fits of laughter.'

He kissed her hair, and went on, 'When I left here after my first visit she came to the airport to see me off. Her eyes were so tearful, big and dark in her made-up face that I felt a pang of pity for her and kissed her gently on her lips. It was a mistake. She kissed me back—and believe me, I had to prise her arms from about my neck. She telephoned me once or twice when I came back, but I treated her as I had done all along, like a benevolent uncle.'

His voice became grim. 'It's only since my return that I learned about her goings-on with other men.'

Sabina thought of Max and realised now that he had been in the same situation as David. There had never been anything serious between him and Shani. It was what she had made of it. David went on.

'Upon our return here I was relieved to know that she was safe with an aunt in Helsinki. I was wrong. She waylaid me each time I went for consultations with Urfo and Skip. I lost my temper with her and told her to lay off or I'd tell her parents. It seemed to work for a while, because then she got in with some students. Remember Bill? He was one. She used to play one off against the other, silly kid.'

'But why didn't you tell me? I would have understood,' she said.

'Would you? If you remember, you were in a funny state of mind after your accident. I had to be very careful with you. It was a miracle that you escaped so lightly. When I think about it . . .' He buried his face in her hair. 'I'm going to need a lot of convincing that I still have you.'

Sabina kissed the hand she held in her own. 'I'm going to make it up to you, my darling.'

Her hands moved blindly to his head caressing it and loving his warm nearness. She was filled with an immeasurable thankfulness that she had not lost him.

Against her hair his lips murmured, 'I'll hold you to that. We have a lot of loving to make up for.'

'We wouldn't have had, if you'd only told me about Shani!' she cried.

'But you didn't know about her—or did you?' A gleam came into his dark eyes when she did not answer. 'Come on, out with it. There has to be complete honesty between us. What happened? It never occurred to me that she would do anything behind my back.'

Sabina told him about Shani coming to see her at the villa soon after they had arrived, and David's face grew murderous as he listened.

'The little so-and-so!' he muttered through clenched teeth. 'You know what she did at the hospital? She was in a car crash in which several of her companions had minor injuries like herself. Only she played up to them, pretending that she had concussion so they would send for me when they heard her repeat my name. The doctors were not amused when they found out her deception. She had me going back to the hospital to be with her.'

'Was that when you asked me not to telephone her parents?'

'The doctors had advised me to wait. They had their

suspicions from the first that she was acting concussed. I went back that night to the hospital and we tricked her into confessing her deception. I was pretty mad by this time, I can tell you. Her aunt was there looking shattered and I could have strangled the little beast. I went home with her aunt and we talked things over. I suggested putting Shani on the first plane we could get the following day to her folks in America. So that's what we did. I helped the aunt to pack Shani's things, took the suitcase to the hospital and escorted her to the airport. She kicked up a fuss until I told her that I wouldn't tell her parents what she'd done if she went to America.'

'My poor David! If only . . .' Sabina murmured.

'Now don't start that again. We aren't going to mention her name again. By the way, Max won't be coming to dress your face today. I told him you and I had things to discuss that were very important.'

'Poor Max. What did he say?'

'Look,' he said, drawing her still closer, 'Max is someone else that we aren't going to talk about. Like Shani, he's taken up far too much of our time.'

'How can you say that about Max when he's done so much for me?' she exclaimed indignantly.

'He erased your scar, so what? I would have loved you just the same, scar and all. I kept telling you that, but you wouldn't believe me.'

'What a lovely compliment!' Her voice was gentle as something lovely and radiant came into her face. Absurd that his deep voice, even when he said things he might or might not mean, should send ripples of joy through her, as if the vibration of his vocal chords struck similar ones in her heart stirring them to melody.

'No compliment,' he contradicted, 'just a statement of

fact. I love you in that kind of way above all else. How do you love me?'

With a tiny amused smile which made her look enchanting she touched his dark intent face. 'I told you.'

He kissed the tip of her nose. 'Tell me again.'

Sabina said them, the irrevocable words, said them with a wonderful joy that made her tremble in his arms. She would have gone on repeating them had not his mouth descended upon her own. Ardent minutes passed. Comfort and blissful happiness washed over her anew and her senses blurred in the magic of his kisses. His hands moved blindly to untie the wrap from around her.

She said quickly, 'David, Blair is here. Did you know?'

'Hmm.'

'He's developing pictures in the sauna house by the lake.'

'Hmm.'

'You're not listening, David . . .'

They were the last words Sabina spoke for quite a long time. The blood surging through her veins was pure magic beneath David's kisses and slowly roused passion. He was the perfect lover as she knew he would be, unhurried as he taught her in the most wonderful way all that marriage meant of love, beauty and happiness.

They were late going down for the evening meal. Sabina floated down in cloudy tulle with her blue eyes no less bright than the necklace of sapphires and ear-rings glittering at her throat and ears. Her hand was tucked in the comforting warmth of David's arm.

He had said with a chuckle, 'The necklace and ear-rings were to have been my gift to you on our wedding night. As it happened, this afternoon I thought it was the appropriate time to give them to you with all my love.'

Sabina was so bemused with happiness that she was not at all surprised to see Kirsty and Blair waiting for them in the salon. It was David who went forward with a purpose to greet Kirsty.

'Thank you for coming to keep Blair in order, Kirsty. Let's all sit down, shall we? This is a rather special occasion,' he said as he served drinks. 'The first stage of the project which brought me here is complete leaving me more time to devote to my beloved wife.' He gave a wicked glance at Sabina as her cheeks took on a warm glow. 'Doesn't she look radiant?'

Blair grinned. 'I'll say she does. I'm going for my camera just now to take a picture. Must have a memento of this happy occasion.'

David gave everybody a glass of champagne and the air scintillated with high spirits as if it was indeed an occasion for rejoicing. Eila and Leif surpassed themselves in the beautifully prepared meal they set before them. They waited on together at the table while the others looked on, Sabina, looking out of this world with the beauty that only true love can bring, David more handsome and vital than ever with a wicked twinkle in his eyes, Kirsty, a little bewildered, sweet and smiling in wild rose silk, and Blair as witty and audacious as ever.

He said, 'You didn't happen to escort a girl to the airport recently, did you, David?'

David's reply came crisp and clear as he looked meaningly at Eila and Leif.

'I did. Miss Shani Somers, to be exact, daughter of the very nice people who have leased us this villa. She's gone to join her parents.'

'Interesting face,' Blair mused. 'Like to give me her telephone number?'

'No, decidedly not. That young woman would prove

too much for even you to handle,' David said grimly.

Kirsty said nothing, but she looked as relieved as Eila and Leif. Sabina felt that the last cloud on her horizon was gone, and with all the generosity of a happy person, she wished there was something she could do to bring the same happiness to Kirsty. They lingered a long time over their coffee, taking it on the terrace overlooking the lake. It came to an unexpected end when Eila came to announce that David and Sabina had a visitor. Immediately David rose, placed firm fingers on Sabina's arm and led her from the terrace with a murmured 'excuse us' back into the room.

Urgently, he whispered, 'Max is here to dress your face, darling. If I know Blair he'll be shooting from the terrace to fetch his camera about the time Max has finished with you. Then Max will be returning to the terrace alone. Can't leave Kirsty on her own, can we?'

For several seconds Sabina stared up into his dark eyes with their now familiar wicked gleam. Then she was aware of Max standing there with his small case.

'David, you darling!' she cried as she comprehended. 'And you, Max, how lovely to see you.'

She tiptoed to give her husband a brief kiss, then bestowed one on Max.

'Hey, now!' David protested. 'No time for that.' But she only laughed.

Everything that happened next was so confused to Sabina that she only fully understood it when recapping the whole events much later with David. This time he was sharing her bed and she lay in his arms.

'What I can't understand is why you didn't tell me about it beforehand.' She gave a deep sigh. 'Wasn't it romantic the way Max strode on to the terrace to grab

Kirsty into his arms? I'm inclined to think you had a hand in that.'

He kissed the tip of her nose and the corners of her mouth hovering into a smile.

Modestly, he admitted, 'I had a talk with Max. I've been jealous of him, you know. So I decided to get him out of your way and mine. As a bachelor he wasn't exactly welcome, although he was attending to your face. You made far too much fuss of him for my liking.'

'Oh, David,' she cried, 'you weren't really jealous?'

He said darkly, 'Just let me catch you going round kissing any of our men friends again and you'll see that I'm not kidding!'

She laughed and kissed the dark frown from his face. 'Tell me more about you acting as Cupid,' she urged.

'Cupid?' he echoed disgustedly. 'I didn't do anything, Max did. Apparently when he went to fetch his mother home after her visit to friends he told her that he was making arrangements to marry Kirsty. He had a special licence and he wanted his mother to be at the wedding.'

Sabina chuckled and felt wicked in doing so. 'Oh, dear! Mrs Hiltunsen wouldn't like that.'

'She didn't. She refused to return home with him until he'd regained his senses. It was sheer bluff on her part that didn't pay off. Max left her in a hotel in Helsinki and came back to make further plans in which we had a part. I invited Kirsty here as a partner for Blair, Max came presumably to attend to your face—and you saw what happened next.'

Sabina smiled dreamily up into his face. 'You saw to everything, didn't you, including the champagne to drink to their engagement? I've never seen Kirsty look so radiantly happy. Did you notice how she kind of sparkles when she laughs? And didn't she look lovely in that wild rose silk dress? Oh, darling, they're going to be wonderfully, ecstatically happy! I do hope Mrs Hiltunsen won't make trouble.'

David chuckled darkly. 'Not a chance. From what Max said she's seeing a lot of a man she met years ago before she was married.'

'I suppose that would be the best way out, for her to marry again. What is Max planning to do?'

'Take his bride away on a long honeymoon like me.'

Sabina shone up at him. 'But we are on honeymoon, aren't we?'

'Not the honeymoon I wanted, away from business and all interference. We're going to Greece to soak up the sun, my sweet. I'm going to dance with you in faraway places, bathe with you in blue, sunny waters, spend ecstatic nights with you under the stars, sit opposite to you at breakfast and adore you . . . and . . .'

'Yes?' she crooned, kissing him sweetly.

He laughed. 'Never you mind. Telling you any more would only spoil it.'

'But we are coming back here, aren't we?'

'Of course. But not to stay here at the villa. I've found a charming villa just outside Helsinki. You'll love it. Only a small place, but big enough to entertain our friends.'

Sabina was starry-eyed. 'Oh, David, how wonderful!'

She had to show him then how grateful she was and how much she loved him. And David lost no time in reciprocating. Together they were embarking on a great adventure in which they would discover each other and all the wonderful things which marriage holds. For Sabina it could not come too soon.

'Love me?' he murmured against her lips.

The pale shimmer of bright blue eyes and tremulous lips flowed up to him to tell him without words what he wanted to know. Deeply moved, he moved his hand caressingly over the rich honey-gold hair, the bared white column of her throat which he had to kiss, and when at last his lips found her mouth Sabina knew that she had everything in life that she had ever wanted in David, her husband.

The Warrender Saga

The most frequently requested Harlequin Romance series

#980 *A Song Begins*

#1100 *The Broken Wing*

#1244 *When Love Is Blind*

#1405 *The Curtain Rises*

#1508 *Child of Music*

#1587 *Music of the Heart*

#1767 *Unbidden Melody*

#1834 *Song Cycle*

#1936 *Remembered Serenade*

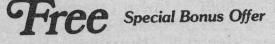

Complete and mail this coupon today!

And there's still *more* love in

Harlequin Presents...

Yes!

Six more spellbinding
romantic stories every month
by your favorite authors.
Elegant and sophisticated tales of
love and love's conflicts.

Let your imagination be swept away to
exotic places in search of adventure,
intrigue and romance. Get to
know the warm, true-to-life
characters. Share the special
kind of miracle that
love can be.

Don't miss out. Buy now and discover
the world of HARLEQUIN PRESENTS...